AD ASTRA

ALSO BY JACK CAMPBELL

THE LOST FLEET

Dauntless
Fearless
Courageous
Valiant
Relentless
Victorious

BEYOND THE FRONTIER

Dreadnaught
Invincible
Guardian
Steadfast
Leviathan

THE LOST STARS

Tarnished Knight
Perilous Shield
Imperfect Sword
Shattered Spear

THE ETHAN STARK SERIES

Stark's War
Stark's Command
Stark's Crusade

THE PAUL SINCLAIR SERIES

A Just Determination
Burden of Proof
Rule of Evidence
Against All Enemies

PILLARS OF REALITY

*The Dragons of Dorcastle**
*The Hidden Masters of Marandur**
*The Assassins of Altis**
*The Pirates of Pacta Servanda**
*The Servants of the Storm**
*The Wrath of the Great Guilds**

NOVELLAS

The Last Full Measure

SHORT STORY COLLECTIONS

*Ad Astra**
*Borrowed Time**
*Swords and Saddles**

*available as a JABberwocky eBook

AD ASTRA

JOHN HEMRY

WRITING AS

JACK CAMPBELL

Published by JABberwocky Literary Agency, Inc.

Ad Astra

This paperback edition published in 2016 by JABberwocky Literary Agency, Inc.

Publication History:

"Lady Be Good" first published in Analog (April, 2006). "As You Know, Bob" first published in Analog (April, 2007). "Do No Harm" first published in Analog (July/August, 2007). "Down the Rabbit Hole" first published in Analog (May, 2001). "Generation Gap" first published in Analog (December, 2002). "Kyrie Eleison" first published in Analog (September, 2006). "Odysseus" first published in Analog (February, 1999). "One Small Spin" first published in Analog (September, 1997). "Section Seven" first published in Analog (September, 2003). "Standards of Success" first published in Analog (March, 2005). "The Bookseller of Bastet" first published in Analog (March, 2008).

Interior design by Estelle Leora Malmed

Cover design by Tiger Bright Studios, Inc.

ISBN 978-1-625672-36-0

CONTENTS

AUTHOR'S NOTE
LADY BE GOOD

One of my favorite writers is Leigh Brackett, who was not only a good science fiction and fantasy author but also worked as a screenwriter in Hollywood, playing a role in films from *The Big Sleep* to *The Empire Strikes Back.* I like her way of writing, and her hard-bitten and wounded heroes (Humphrey Bogart was a particular favorite of hers, which is why Han Solo in *Empire* takes on the depth of one of Bogart's characters). Something else that had always fascinated me was the saga of a US bomber named *Lady Be Good* which had vanished in 1943, only to be discovered intact in the Libyan desert in 1959. Her crew had died within days from heat and lack of water, but the bomber had remained as an silent memorial to them, perfectly preserved. I wanted to write about that, but not simply retelling that story. I wanted something about sacrifice, but also achievement. One day I started writing this story, and it flowed out as if Leigh herself was whispering the words to me. I think it's one of the best stories I've written. *Lady Be Good* won the Analog magazine a*ward f*or best novelette of 2006.

LADY BE GOOD

There's a place, they say, where sailors go when their last voyage ends, when their ships come apart among the drifting reefs of an asteroid belt or vanish in the great dark between the stars that light worlds. A place where the engines never falter and the hull never cracks, where particle storms never rage in sudden fury that pierces shielding to shred the workings of machines and men and leave lifeless wrecks in their wake. A place where every sailor has a safe posting and a fair wage and every Captain sees a decent profit from a hard run. A place where the bars are cheap and honest, the planet-tied greet sailors with open hands and hearts, and every ship finds welcome and a safe berth.

The place is called Haven, they say. No chart shows you the way, no sailing directions offer guidance, no star map carries the name. But when the need is great and the time is right, a true sailor will find it. Or so they say.

"Bunch 'a crap," Dingo mumbled around his beer mug as the old drunk at the next table kept talking about the mythical sailor's paradise known as Haven. Dingo drained the last of the brew and banged his now-empty mug on the table. A passing waiter paused just long-enough to slop more beer into the mug, allowing a big head to form, and tapped the counter on his waist racking up Dingo's tab. Dingo grunted with disgust and blew off the foam, squinting at the actual beer level. "They do that on purpose."

"Really?" I pushed a lot of sarcasm into the word so that even Dingo would pick up on it. "When'd you figure that out?"

"Go to hell, First Officer Kilcannon, *sir*," Dingo suggested. "They're cheating us, is what they're doin'."

"And they do the same damn thing in every damn bar in every damn port from here all the way back to Mother Sol."

Dingo drained his beer again, belched, and got another partial 'refill' almost as fast. "That's what I mean. That attitude. What makes them think they can get away with that?"

"Experience with dumb sailors."

"Screw you, Kilcannon."

"No, thanks. I've already had that taken care of today."

"Then why're you bein' such a wise-ass? Wasn't it any fun?"

I shrugged. "It was business. Services paid for, services provided."

"Saints, but ain't you in a foul mood. Have another beer." Dingo flopped backward and smiled loosely. "Works every time."

It did for Dingo, anyway. I looked at him, sagging into his battered chair, his eyes glazing over as the alcohol from several earlier beers finally hit his system. Dingo didn't believe in Haven, maybe because he thought he could find it in every bar. As long as his money held out and I got his drunken carcass back to the ship afterwards. "Don't forget we're sailing tomorrow."

"Why do you think I'm getting this drunk?" Dingo stared blearily at his beer mug, as if uncertain whether it still held liquid.

"I'm going to need you functioning tomorrow. We've got three new hands coming onboard."

"Hah! How'd you swing that? Lie about our next port?"

"Yeah."

Dingo began laughing silently, his sides shaking and an enormous grin splitting his face. He bent over, gasping for air. "They'll kill ya when they find out, Kilcannon," he finally managed to stammer. "I swear they'll kill ya."

"I'll worry about that when the time comes."

"You do that." Dingo raised his mug, tipping it vertical to get every drop. It fell back onto the table again but before the waiter could slosh any more into the mug I slapped his hand aside. "Hey. I ain't done."

"Yes, you are."

"You ain't my mother and you ain't the Captain and dammed if I'll let you nursemaid me, Kilcannon! I quit!" Dingo struggled to his feet, his hands clenched into fists. I stayed seated, just looking back at him. "Get up! Damn ya, get up! When I'm done there won't be enough of ya left to run through a recycler."

"Right." I stood slowly, keeping my hands lowered. "Let's go."

"I told you I quit! I ain't goin' on this voyage! I never aimed to and I won't! Not there!"

"Okay."

My answer took a moment to penetrate through layers of alcohol-soaked brain cells, then Dingo lowered his fists a little and stared at me. "Okay?"

"Sure. Let's get your stuff off the ship. You'll need it."

Dingo grinned broadly, wavering on his feet. "Now that's a saintly way to be, Kilcannon. I was wrong about you. Sure I was."

I plopped a credit chip on the table and steered Dingo out of the bar. We wended our way back to the ship, dodging other drunk sailors as we went. Every once in a while, the orbital port's gravity would stutter a little in our area, making me waver on my feet as badly as Dingo for a moment. That's one of the hazards of being in the low-rent areas of any port off-planet. Outside every bar in the area near the port were other hazards, men and women who looked young and cheap and pretty in the dim lighting, beckoning and calling invitations to visit the particular establishments where they got kick-backs for luring in customers. I fended off all of them.

Our IDs got us onto the pier and onto the ship. Dingo paused outside his quarters, swaying on his feet as if our ship was riding on a planetary ocean. "Ya sure this is okay, Kilcannon?"

"Yeah. No problem."

"I'm gonna get my kit."

"You do that." I gestured him inside. Dingo grinned and staggered into his quarters. I waited until he was almost to the bunk, then keyed in the security override on the hatch. Dingo was still turning his head to see what the noise was when the hatch slid shut and locked. I heard a roar of anger, followed a second later by the impact of Dingo's body against the hatch. Silence followed, so apparently Dingo had knocked himself out. Hopefully he wasn't hurt too badly. I had no intention of cracking that hatch before the ship was safely underway tomorrow. "See you in the morning, Third Officer Dingo."

I walked down the passageway, easily seeing dark patches of mold on the overhead even in the dimmed night lighting of the ship. The *Lady Be Good* badly needed a full-scale fumigation, but that was just one of the things she badly needed that she wasn't going to get any time soon.

* * *

The port inspector arrived half an hour late to give us departure clearance. As far as I knew, Dingo still hadn't awoken and started demanding his freedom, and none of the three new sailors had shown any signs they suspected our destination wasn't the same one they'd signed on for. The inspector gave the entry lock of the Lady a sour look., but she couldn't flunk us on the basis of that lock. I kept that working even if it wasn't pretty.

The inspector ran down the checklist. "You claim you've signed on enough new sailors to meet minimum crew requirements."

"That's right." You couldn't be too subservient or the public servants would ride right over you, but you couldn't dis 'em either. Not if you were smart. "You can confirm they're onboard from the pier access records."

"There's ways to gimmick those records."

"I wouldn't know anything about that."

"I bet you don't." She picked a name at random. "I want to see Able Spacer Kanidu. In person. Here."

"Okay." Odds had favored her picking one of the new hires, but I'd still worried she might ask to see Dingo. Dingo would come around once we were underway. He always did after any little misunderstandings while he was drunk. But right now he'd still be a bit upset with me.

Kanidu answered the hail quick enough. Short and stout, she gave the inspector a bland look and confirmed all of her qualification data. Finally satisfied, the inspector let the sailor go. "I need to verify your cargo manifest."

"Sure." I let her plug into the ship systems and check the cargo containers. A really good inspector would've suited up and crawled over the big cargo containers fastened around Lady's core, even opening the loading doors to check that the contents matched the manifests. But really good inspectors didn't work the early morning weekend shifts and didn't bother with small freighters like *Lady*, so it'd been safe to assume we'd just get a manifest check.

I'd been assured the inspector wouldn't be able to spot that the manifests had been falsified. I mentally crossed my fingers and hoped the assurances were accurate.

Apparently they were. The inspector moved on to more items on the checklist, mostly dealing with equipment. "It's been a long time since your last engine certification."

"We're within limits."

"Time-wise, maybe." She gave the entry lock another look. "How well does your gear still work?"

It wouldn't take a lot of experience for her to guess our gear wouldn't pass a certification test right now. "It works fine."

"Maybe I ought to look at it."

Maybe. I knew what that meant. "Hey, I just remembered something. Can you hold here just a sec?"

She gave her watch an annoyed look and nodded. I went straight to my quarters. In the bottom of one drawer, well wrapped, I found the bottle and carefully carried it out. "I've got a friend in port I meant to give this. But I forgot. Could you get it to him?"

"I suppose." She took the bribe, examining the label as if ready to reject it, but then her face cleared. "From Mother Sol?"

"Yeah." Mother Sol was a long, long ways from the port of Mandalay orbiting the planet of the same name orbiting the star humans had named Ganesha. Anything from Sol, even rotgut, had the exotic aura imbued by great distance, and this wasn't rotgut. "From Martinique. That's an island. It's good rum. You ought to try some."

"Maybe I will. I guess this friend isn't that special if this is all you got him."

I shrugged and gestured at the entry lock. "Funds are pretty short right now. It's all I could afford."

"Okay." Cover story for the bribe established for the benefit of any hidden recorders, and her questioning whether we could give her a bigger pay off also fielded, the inspector pocketed the bottle. "You're cleared for departure. But I've tagged your ship entry. Next time you hit this port you'd better have a recent engine certification or we'll do a full inspection."

"No problem."

She grinned at what we both knew was a lie, then headed off, patting the place where she'd stashed that rum. Damn. I'd been saving it for a special occasion. But like just about everything else I'd had to use it in an emergency.

I checked the lock's log to confirm everyone was aboard, then sealed the lock tight. "Able Spacers Kanidu, Jungo, and Siri. Meet me in the crews mess."

The two tables grandly labeled the crews mess had plenty of empty places even when breakfast was supposedly being handed out. Dingo wasn't here, of course, but we had a lot of unfilled slots. We couldn't afford to pay for a full crew, but then again that wasn't really a problem because it was so hard to get sailors to sign on to a ship in *Lady's* shape that recruiting just enough to meet minimum standards was a big enough challenge.

Kanidu eyed me in a disinterested way as I assigned her to engineering and pointed her toward Chief Engineer Vox at one of the tables. Vox just nodded silently when Kanidu reported to her.

Jungo was a tall, slim guy with an eager smile who'd been happy to sign on. I wondered what he was hiding and who or what he was running from. I gave him to the cargo section.

Last came Siri. She was a small woman, thin and shivering slightly, carrying every indication of being a star dust addict. No wonder no other ship had taken her on. She'd go cold turkey for certain on our voyage, which wouldn't be pretty, but the worst that could happen was she'd die and then we wouldn't have to pay her. I gave her to ship's systems, because she'd been certified a System Tech Second Rate at one point. Maybe her dust-addled brain still remembered some of that.

I stopped next to the Chief Engineer. "We okay to go?"

Vox nodded wordlessly again.

"Anything I need to tell the Captain?"

Vox dug something out from between her teeth before answering. "Refit."

"I know we need a refit. As soon as I can -."

"Shipyard."

I stopped talking and just nodded back. The *Lady* needed a full engineering refit in a shipyard, nothing less. The Chief Engineer had a responsibility to remind me of that. I couldn't do a thing about it, but I had to be reminded of it.

I went forward, trying to figure out where I might be able to get the Lady's engines looked at for something less than cut-rate prices. Maybe an under-used maintenance facility at a middle-of-nowhere star would be willing to give us a break for the sake of keeping their hands in. It was worth a try.

Captain Jane Weskind sat in her still-darkened cabin. She'd

gotten dressed by herself but didn't look good this morning. "We're cleared to leave," I reported, standing in front of her desk and touching my brow with my right hand.

A long moment passed. Weskind's face cycled through a half-dozen emotions before she caught it and froze it in a shaky grin. "No problems?" It was what she always said, now.

There wasn't a thing she could do about engineering and she'd already been told we were overdue for a yard period. "No problems."

"Good work, First Officer Kilcannon." She lowered her voice, as if sharing a secret. "The *Lady* needs work. I know it." A long pause. "A good profit on this run. That's all we need. One good run." Another pause. "Right, Kilcannon?"

"Right, Captain." She always said that, too. Just one good run. That wouldn't be enough, of course, but with the profit from one good run we could set up an even better run and then we'd be on our way up again. Dingo might think Haven was in the nearest bar but Captain Weskind clung to it being one good run away. It seemed it had always been one good run away and maybe it always would be one good run away. Maybe not, though. This run did promise a good return. Not without risk, of course. I smiled and nodded at Captain Weskind's words because this really could be the one good run we needed, and because I was sure Captain Weskind needed to believe that run would happen and needed to know I believed it, too. "Will you be on the bridge when we leave port, Captain?"

More expressions chased their way across Captain Weskind's face. "I…have work, First Officer Kilcannon."

"I understand, Captain. I'll take the ship out."

"Thank you, First Officer Kilcannon."

I saluted again and left, making sure her hatch was set to notify me if Captain Weskind left her cabin. It didn't happen much nowadays, but I needed to be there if she needed me.

Leaving port was the usual mix of tension and boredom. Tension because things could go wrong. A blown directional vector or an aging control system sending the wrong commands could result in a painful meeting of ship and some other object. *Lady* wasn't the smallest freighter running between stars, but she wasn't all that big, either. Odds were if we hit anything *Lady* would be the loser.

But it was boring, too, because the procedures were ones we'd run through a hundred times and they didn't change all that much from port to port. Same old drill, often in different places, but always the same old drill.

Then we were out of the confines of the port and running free down the outbound shipping lanes, heading outward past planets and rocks and comets, aiming to get far enough from the gravity well of Mandalay's sun Ganesha to start our jump. Systems, especially inner systems, always felt cramped and crowded when you were used to the wide open freedom of the big dark. Nearly a hundred suns held human colonies now, and even after so many years of sailing between them I still felt a moment of wonder at the thought that the *Lady* could carry me to any sun and planet I chose. In theory. In practice, we could only go where the paying cargo runs took us. The roads between the stars aren't free, no matter what the poets dream far away on Mother Sol.

Here, close to port, the inbound lanes passed near the outbound. I watched the big ships coming in. Sol Transport, Vestral Shipping, Combined Systems, Great Spinward. The ships belonging to the giant companies seemed to glow on our screens, all their systems registering in top shape on our read-outs. I fought down a wave of envious anger. With a fraction of what the big companies spent to keep those ships of theirs shiny I could get *Lady* back in shape. But it wouldn't happen. *Lady* was beneath their attention. The ports *Lady* called at were often beneath their attention. The cargo *Lady* carried usually wasn't worth it for the big carriers. So I watched the big ships pass and wished for more of their leavings.

Maybe some of them were watching old, small, battered *Lady* heading out. If they were watching, I could too easily imagine what they were thinking. I wished the wrath of the saints on smug company spacers and went to let Dingo out of his quarters.

* * *

I double-checked the jump solution while Dingo glared at me. The lump visible on his forehead hadn't aided his forgiving me for tricking him last night. But he'd done his job right. A short run to Wayfare, then a middling run to a nowhere star named Carnavon that didn't see much traffic and wouldn't have any local authorities asking awkward questions, and finally a long run into Fagin. The circuitous route should bring us into Fagin along routes a fair ways from the usual inbound and outbound channels for that system. "Looks good."

"As if I didn't know this job better'n you, Kilcannon!"

"Dingo, somebody has to double-check things like this. You know that, too."

"Oh, I know lots, Kilcannon. Did you tell them new ones yet where we're goin'?"

"No." Jungo, nearby, looked over with ill-conceal alarm.

Dingo grinned nastily. "Where d'they *think* we're goin'?"

I didn't answer, so Dingo looked at Jungo, who swallowed nervously. "Polder," he half-whispered.

"Polder! Hah! Try Fagin, lad."

"Fagin?" Jungo paled. "But…the war."

"Yeah! Civil war! Brother against brother! The best kind. And the best rates for those willing to try to run cargo in through the privateers roamin' the spaceways."

The crew would've heard sooner or later, but I still wasn't happy having it spilled now, days before we'd get far enough out-system to enter jump to Wayfare. "Shut up."

Dingo just grinned at me. "'Shut up,' is it? And what'll you do if I don't, Kilcannon? Shanghai me on a voyage to a war zone in an old tub that should've seen the wrecker's yard a handful of years ago?"

Jungo was shaking his head. "I signed on for Polder." His voice wavered. "My contract says Polder."

I shook my own head. "Your contract contains a necessity clause which allows the ship to change destinations if required. You ought to be grateful for that. We won't meet any arrest warrants on any of our crew that've been forwarded to Polder. Right?"

Dingo laughed again, Jungo looked stricken and relieved at the same time, and I ignored both of them.

* * *

So many ships. I keyed the transmitter again. "Wayfare System Control, this is *Lady Be Good* still awaiting authorization to clear system."

I sat back to wait. Spacer Siri was at the auxiliary control panel on the bridge, shivering constantly, her eyes going into and out of focus. Withdrawal from star dust wasn't pleasant to watch, but watching was all anyone on the *Lady* could do. It'd either kill her or leave her clear. So far, Siri had been able to follow orders when I snapped them at her.

A babble of messages from other ships to Wayfare System Control and each other flowed in after I stopped transmitting. The authorities at Wayfare were obviously overwhelmed again. Why one of the most often used relay stars couldn't upgrade its system control was beyond me.

Lady was skating along the fringes of Wayfare, just heading for the jump point to Carnavon. A slightly unusual route, but I knew from experience that Wayfare System Control would be too busy to worry about what one little freighter was up to.

And I was right. "*Lady Be Good*, authorization granted to clear Wayfare." I punched in the jump commands, secure in the knowledge nobody was paying attention to *Lady*.

Nearby, Spacer Siri shivered. I dug a packet out of one of my pockets and tossed it to her. "These'll help." She caught the packet automatically and stared at it. "Somebody I knew beat star dust. They said that stuff helped a lot."

Siri nodded, tearing open the packet with trembling hands. I went back to studying my control panel. Somewhere aft, one of the engines groaned into momentary instability that made my stomach flutter. A moment later, Chief Engineer Vox called the bridge. "Bad."

"Can you hold it together?"

"Yeah."

"How long?"

"Depends."

"Give me as much warning as you can."

"Just did."

* * *

Carnavon was small and dim. For a star, that is. No other ship beacons flared on our scans. Quiet and isolated, just the place for a small ship looking to avoid awkward questions.

To get the right arrival angle on Fagin we'd have to fall through the Carnavon system and climb out the other side, a time-consuming pain in the neck under any circumstances.

"Hey, Kilcannon."

"What, Dingo?"

"On the bridge, sweetheart."

I made my way up there, wondering what Dingo could have to talk about that needed me on the bridge in person. Most of the possibilities weren't very good. But Dingo didn't seem worried as he pointed at scan. "What d'ya think that is, Kilcannon?"

I peered at it, checked readings, then thought about it. "What do you think it is?"

"I asked first." Dingo smiled with derision. "Don't know, d'ya? How long ya been a sailor, Kilcannon?"

"Long enough." I frowned at the scan. "It looks like a dead ship."

"Not bad! It's a ship, alright." Dingo's smile vanished. "She ain't dead. Not yet." He tapped a blunt nail on some of the readouts. "It's real faint, but there's still a heat source active in there, and leaking atmosphere."

"Saints. Are you saying there's someone still alive on that thing?"

"Could be."

A wreck would've been interesting as a possible source of parts, though probably not interesting enough to warrant a diversion from our course. Wrecks tended to be stripped before we ever saw them. But if some of the crew had holed up in the interior... "There's no distress beacon."

"Nah. Which tells you and me how that wreck got in trouble, right?" I immediately checked scan again, but Dingo was already grinning at me. "I checked. As good as I could with this tub's instruments. There ain't no other ships burning engines in this system right now. Either the pirates or privateers are sitting quiet in ambush, or they've left."

I scowled at the display. "Getting to that wreck will take us way off our track."

"Yeah."

"If somebody was waiting to ambush any rescuers, they'd have left the distress beacon working to lure people in, wouldn't they?"

"Yeah."

"But anybody still onboard it is most likely already dead."

"Yeah."

"But if anyone finds out we disregarded a ship in distress they'll take the *Lady* and our licenses."

"Yeah. But if any survivors die they won't be telling on us, will they?"

"Damn you, Dingo. Get us over to that thing." I turned away. "I'll brief the Captain."

"Yeah. You do that."

* * *

It was a big one. Once *Lady* got close enough we could read the registry. *Canopus Rising*, one of the Vestral Company's ships. But she wasn't bright and pretty anymore. Somebody had kicked *Canopus Rising* in the butt and kept kicking.

"Engines slagged," Chief Engineer Vox grunted, pointing to the image. Somebody had hit that part of the *Canopus* with heavy artillery while the engines were running, adding the suddenly unleashed power of the ship's own engines to the destruction the weapon wrought.

I exhaled as a slim hope vanished. "What're the chances any parts in those engineering areas are salvageable?"

"Zilch."

I brought us as close as I could. We were still picking up faint leakage of heat and gases, so whatever survival space the crew must have rigged up still existed. Whether there was anyone left alive in it was another matter. "Dingo, take the lifeboat over. Take three sailors along to help."

"You're not going yourself?"

I gave Dingo a level stare. "I have to stay with the ship. And keep the Captain informed."

"Ah, yes, so you do. Can you walk with me to the lifeboat?" I went along, knowing Dingo wanted to say something where we couldn't be overheard. "Kilcannon, there's a chance they're still alive, and if they're still alive, there's a chance they're in bad shape, and if they're in bad shape then there ain't much you or I can do for them."

I pretended to study the read-outs on the lifeboat access. "And?"

"Do we haul 'em here and wake 'em up enough to know they're hurting so they can die?"

I took a deep breath, thinking. "Yes."

Dingo shrugged. "You're the boss."

"Dingo, it's up to the saints whether or not they die. I won't make that decision for them."

Another grin. "The saints don't like to be crossed, do they? Ah, here's my crew. Strap in."

I reported to Captain Weskind, then went back to the bridge and watched the lifeboat match velocity, roll and tumble to the wreck. Whatever his limitations as a man of culture, Dingo was a sailor's sailor who knew how to drive even a lumbering lifeboat.

I'd learned patience on many long watches between the stars, and I needed it now. I knew Dingo and his crew were working their way inside the wrecked ship, but Lady couldn't afford fancy communications and tracking gear. All I could do was watch the lifeboat where it rested on the hull of the *Canopus* and wait.

It took an hour. "Ahoy on the *Lady*, this is Third Officer Dingo."

"This is Kilcannon."

"We got 'em. Six souls. They're all walkin'."

Six sailors. Maybe Vestral would cough up a reward. "Anything we can use onboard?"

"Nah. The bastards who done 'er in stripped 'er good. All we're gettin' out of this one is happy points with the saints."

"Most likely." Perhaps ten more minutes passed, then the lifeboat detached from the wreck and made its slow way back.

I was at the access when they arrived. Curiosity aside, protocol demanded it and I wasn't going to let any company sailors say the *Lady* hadn't done things right.

Two officers, three able spacers, and one woman who wasn't wearing a crew coverall. The senior officer extended his hand to me. "First Officer Chen. We'd about given up hope."

I shook his hand and smiled politely. "I'm glad we were able to help." Behind Chen, the junior company spacers were gaping around in obvious dismay at the condition of the *Lady*. The other officer and the woman showed better manners.

Chen gestured to his companion. "Third Officer Constantine." Constantine nodded her head, giving me a grateful smile.

Then Chen pointed to the woman who wasn't dressed like crew, but before he could speak she came forward. "Halley Keracides. Thank you, Captain."

I shook my head. "I'm First Officer Kilcannon. Captain Weskind couldn't be here. She sends her apologies. What happened to you all?"

Chen grimaced. "When we came out of jump here in Carnavon there was a pirate right on top of us." Dingo frowned in disbelief. I imagine I did, too. "I know the odds against that. But it turned out our Fourth Officer had sold our jump calculations. Perfect place to betray us, a system where the odds of anyone stumbling across the attack would be almost zero."

"I take it that's why the Fourth Officer's not with you."

Another grimace. "Him because he sold us out, and most of the others for ransom from Vestral. But the pirates didn't have enough space for all of us, they said, so they left us six behind. Me and Constantine with the sailors because they said we had bad attitudes."

I imagined the Captain of the *Canopus* had displayed plenty of bad attitude as well, but they would've needed him or her for any ransom demand. I looked at Halley Keracides. Neither she nor her clothes bore signs of anything beyond a middle-class income. "I guess they didn't think Vestral would cough up any money for you."

She gave me a flat look back. "Why would they?"

Then again, maybe she'd had a bad attitude, too. I faced First Officer Chen. "Our crew's not at full strength so we've got some spare accommodations. You can have our Second Officer's quarters."

Chen nodded politely, keeping whatever thoughts he might have to himself about a ship that was sailing without a Second Officer onboard. "Thank you for the offer, but I feel Ms. Keracides should have those quarters."

It didn't matter to me. "Fine. Dingo, show everyone to their quarters."

"I got a lifeboat to stow, darlin'." I counted to five slowly, letting

Dingo see how I felt. He shrugged. "Fine. I'll do it later. Come on, you."

Chen must have talked to his sailors, because the next time I saw them they were pretending not to notice what bad shape the *Lady* was in. Chen offered on behalf of all the sailors to work for their room and board until I could drop them off in port, which offer I cheerfully accepted. I could use skilled sailors, especially ones I didn't have to pay. "What about Ms. Keracides? What's she do?"

Chen dropped his eyes and shrugged. "She's a manager of some sort, I understand."

"Then she doesn't do much."

This time, Chen grinned. "Probably not. Uh, I don't want to imply anything, but I do know something about engineering..."

"Our system's badly in need of overhaul. I know."

"I might be able to help. I asked your Chief Engineer about it, but she didn't say anything."

"She usually doesn't," I advised Chen. "Just show up and do whatever you can."

I was on the bridge, picking at my lunch, when Halley Keracides came up. She peered around. It wasn't the blank surface examination of someone out of their depth, though. She apparently knew something about ships. "Mind if I sit down?" she asked.

I indicated the observer's chair. "Feel free."

She twisted the chair, giving me an arch look as it protested swiveling. "I wanted to thank you again. It was getting very bad in the survival compartment the crew had rigged up. I was getting ready to greet the saints."

I nodded. "You're welcome."

"Where are we going?"

I'd been waiting for that question, but I guess Chen had been hesitant to ask. I balanced truth and falsehood for a moment in my mind and decided the truth didn't matter at this point. "Fagin."

"Fagin?" she questioned. Then she repeated it, her voice sharper. "*Fagin?*"

"Yeah, Fagin."

"That's a war zone."

"That's why we're getting paid well to run this cargo in."

She watched me for a moment. "Why are you going to Fagin through Carnavon?"

So Ms. Keracides really did know something about ships. Or about the routes ships took between stars, anyway. "We needed a different approach path in-system." I couldn't tell how much she understood what that implied.

Her eyes narrowed. "You'll be out of normal transit lanes."

She understood a lot. "We want to avoid privateers. All three sides in the civil war have issued letters of marque."

"You'll also be avoiding peacekeepers, won't you?"

She understood entirely too much. "It's a calculated risk. Perhaps you're unaware of the realities of operating for a ship like the *Lady*. We don't have company contacts and company contracts. We get by on what the big companies don't want to bother with. That means we end up taking chances."

"There's nothing dishonorable about working a smaller ship," she stated, answering the thing I hadn't said.

"No, Ms. Keracides, there isn't. I'm sorry we're taking you into Fagin. But once we drop off our cargo we'll be able to get you to a peacekeeper station. Vestral ships help supply those, right? So you'll be okay. It'd only take a few more weeks to pass through Carnavon, then a little while in jump."

"We appreciate the service, First Officer Kilcannon," she stated dryly.

After Halley Keracides had left, I wondered for a moment why she'd lumped herself in with the Vestral employees with that 'we.'

* * *

A week later to the day, Halley Keracides was leaning against the entry to my quarters, her arms crossed over her chest. "I just learned a funny thing."

I sighed and leaned back to look at her. "What's that?"

"First Officer Chen saw a part in your engine room that looked a lot like something Vestral uses. Proprietary design. It'd been modified to fit your system."

I pretended to think about that. "So?"

"Vestral doesn't sell those parts. Where'd you get it?"

"A bulk salvage supplier. He gave us a clean bill on it."

"Uh huh. What'd he charge?"

I let annoyance show. "I'd have to look that up."

"Don't bother. I bet it was fairly cheap, right?"

I stared down at my desk. "We could afford it. The supplier gave us a clean bill."

"Kilcannon, I'm not an idiot and neither are you. That part was obviously stolen property."

I looked back at her, keeping my expression controlled. "The supplier gave us a clean bill," I repeated.

"And you expect me to believe that you never suspected the part was stolen."

"I'm not a cop and I don't have the time or money to do the cops' jobs for them."

"An ethical sailor wouldn't do that kind of business," she shot back.

"Some kinds of ethics are luxuries, Ms. Keracides. We can't afford a lot of luxuries on the *Lady*."

Her face closed down and she started to spin away, then stopped herself and eyed me. "'*Some* kinds of ethics are luxuries,' you said. Just some kinds?"

"Other kinds are necessities. I haven't forgotten that." I rubbed my lower face with one hand, looking away from her again. "I believe I'm still an honest person, Ms. Keracides. And I know the

Lady is still an honest ship. Captain Weskind wouldn't have it any other way."

"I'll have to take your word for that, since I've yet to meet her."

"I'll try to set up a meeting."

"Thank you." She was silent for a long time, and when I finally looked back at my entry I saw she'd gone.

* * *

Two days shy of jump I felt the shock of something, then the *Lady* shuddered and bucked. I was halfway to the bridge before the motion damped out. One scan of the instruments told me where the problem was. "Engineering? Are you okay down there?"

"Yeah."

"What the hell was that?"

Chen came on. "The primary waste heat vent has blown."

I dug my knuckles into my head, trying to think. The engines couldn't run long with the primary vent out. If we didn't get it fixed soon the engines would overheat. Then we either let them blow or shut them down, in which case the radiation shields would drop and the high-energy particles being hurled out by Carnavon would fry us in short order. Unlike the *Canopus*, the *Lady* didn't have a radiation-shielded citadel where we could hide for a while. "How long to fix?"

"You tell me. That's an external job. What shape is your external repair 'bot in?"

I almost laughed at the question. "External repair 'bots are for company ships. Ships like the *Lady* can't afford that stuff."

Chen took a moment to answer. "You'll need to send a sailor out. It's hazardous, but there's no alternative"

"Yeah."

"He or she has to know the equipment and how to replace the vent and be qualified for external repairs underway. I'm afraid my own sailors don't know your layout well enough."

"I wasn't going to volunteer them." Maybe my reply had come

out harsh. Chen didn't talk again for a while. "There's a couple of people on *Lady* who can do it." Yeah. Two of us.

Fifteen minutes later, Dingo checked the last seals on his suit and gave me a lop-sided grin. "Gonna make me earn my pay this time out, eh?"

I tried to smile back. "You know how to do this, Dingo. Better than anyone else on the ship. I talked to the Captain and we agreed you were the only one who could do it."

"Yeah. Sure. You're gonna keep them engines goin' while I'm out there, ain't ya?"

"We don't have any choice."

"Gonna be no fun, Kilcannon. Not hangin' on the outside while the engines are goin' and me wrestling with that duct."

I nodded. "I swear, Dingo, I'd go if I could."

"If something happens to me before I finish the job you'll *have* to go. And good luck trying to finish it yourself. You're not half the outer hull rider that I am. Not half the sailor, neither, though you'll never admit it. Tell you what, Kilcannon, when we hit the next port you pay for the beers. And no bitchin' from you on account I'll be drinkin' the good stuff. Deal?"

"Deal."

"And if worst comes to worst, you put in a good word with the saints for me."

"I'll do that."

I watched the lock mechanism cycle, not knowing what else I could do, while Dingo exited the lock and headed aft along the outer hull. At some point I realized Halley Keracides had come up to stand nearby. "I understand the primary waste heat vent blew," she stated softly.

"Yeah."

"I've never heard if that happening."

I gave her an icy stare. "Not on a Vestral ship, I'm sure. But if you go long enough between engine overhauls it can happen."

"Saints, Kilcannon, it takes more than a missed overhaul to lose a primary waste heat vent."

She was right, which made me wonder again just what kind of 'manager' Halley Keracides really was. "The part was reworked. We got it quite a while back."

Her voice stayed soft. "That's one hell of a way to keep a ship running, Kilcannon."

"It's the only way I've got."

Instead of answering she just stared at the airlock controls along with me. In my mind, I traced the path Dingo would be taking, out the airlock and crawling up over the last row of cargo containers strapped around *Lady* like a huge belt. The containers that came carrying our cargo tended to be old and poorly maintained, so handholds were often loose or missing entirely. After getting over that obstacle, he'd have to work his way back down onto *Lady*'s hull to where the vents lay not far from the stern. Even in dock the trip could be a pain in the neck. Out here it'd be, as Dingo had said, no fun at all.

Given that, I wasn't surprised it took another couple of minutes before Dingo called in. "Hey, on the *Lady*. You there, Kilcannon?"

"I'm here. How's it look?"

"Like hell's own mess."

"Can you fix it?"

"If I can't, no one can."

As the minutes crawled by I tried not to think about Dingo out there on the hull, the energies of the engines thundering not far from him. Even the tightest grip on a hull felt too light when your ship was running through the dark. But Dingo would have to anchor himself using tethers and employ both hands to replace the failed sections of the vent, wrestling with warped metal in the dark and the cold, wearing a suit I knew was too old and too worn. "Dingo."

"Waddaya want?" Dingo sounded out of breath. Tired.

"Maybe I should swap out with you."

"Hell, no. It's almost done."

I checked with engineering. "We've got thirty minutes until shut off will be required. That's plenty of time for you to get in here and rest and me to take care of what's left to do."

"Not your bloody damned job, Kilcannon! Shut up and let me work. It's almost done."

Halley gave me a questioning look and I shrugged. I couldn't go out and drag him back. We waited.

"Almost." Dingo's voice sounded ragged now.

"Kilcannon, this is Chen in engineering. We're getting a heat spike."

Whichever saint had been watching us had just looked away. "Dingo, drop it and get inside. Now. We've got a heat spike."

"I drop it now and we'll lose it."

"That's an order, Third Officer Dingo."

"Didn't hear it."

"Kilcannon, this is Chen. We have to vent that spike. We're holding down the overrides, but the safeties won't let us do that much longer. If the heat spike vents through the secondary it may blow."

"Dingo, damn you -."

"Got it!"

"The safeties overrode our commands! They're dumping the spike!"

"Dingo!" Lady shuddered again. I waited a long moment. "Dingo. Third Officer Dingo. Respond." Halley Keracides had her eyes hidden behind one hand. "Third Officer Dingo. Respond." I grabbed the other suit and started getting into it. "Dingo. By all the saints, Dingo…"

I'd never realized how slowly the airlock cycled. I couldn't feel anything, including fear, but out of force of habit I made my way cautiously over the battered cargo containers and along the hull as I moved toward the vent. I found Dingo still tethered there. The emergency vent through the secondary had blown away part of its shield, and some of those parts had gone through Dingo's suit and Dingo on their way to forever.

I checked the work on the vent. Dingo had done a good job. Better than I could've done. Then I untethered all that remained of my Third Officer and towed him back to the airlock.

There was a group waiting at the airlock. Dingo had never been a particularly good-looking man. Explosive decompression hadn't improved things any. "Let's get him into the burial capsule." I'd kept one. I could've hocked it, like I had the others, but was afraid if I got rid of the last one I'd suddenly need it. Now I needed it anyway.

The other sailors wrestled Dingo's body into the capsule. "Drop it into the cold storage bin. We'll hold a service later and send it toward Carnavon." I watched them carry the capsule away, wondering what I'd say at the service.

Halley stood watching me. "Did he have any friends?"

"Who? Dingo? No."

"You're sure? Nobody he went ashore with?"

I managed a short, sharp bark of laughter. "I'm the only one who ever went ashore with Dingo."

"Really?"

"Yeah." I rubbed my forehead, trying to push away the pain there. "Dingo was a drunk, and he'd usually get mean."

"Why'd you go with him, then?"

"Somebody had to. Somebody had to make sure he was okay and get him back to the ship."

"You could've told someone else to do it."

I frowned and shook my head. "No. I couldn't trust anyone else not to ditch Dingo when he started getting mean drunk. And it was just easier for me to keep an eye on him." I looked up and saw Halley still watching me. "What?"

"I was just thinking that Dingo did have one friend. And I think he knew it, too."

I shrugged. "And I was just thinking that I wish I'd checked Dingo's suit before we sealed that capsule to see if it could be repaired."

I don't know what kind of reaction I was expecting from her, but Halley Keracides just shook her head. "You're a damned liar, Kilcannon." Then she walked away and left me standing there alone at the airlock.

* * *

We made it the next two days without further problems. Before *Lady* jumped for Fagin, I held a brief service for Dingo, going over the standard burial in space service and saying some things that were true, like he'd been one hell of a sailor, and some things that weren't so true, like he'd also been one hell of a human being. But the saints expected praise when we sent them a new spirit and Dingo deserved whatever boost I could give him.

The burial capsule dropped back toward Carnavon as we accelerated to jump. In time, Dingo's body would be cremated in the fires of that sun. There are worse grave markers.

It'd be a long run to Fagin, with nothing to do but hope nothing else really important broke. I briefed Captain Weskind again. She told me we just needed one good run. I agreed. It looked like we might finally be getting that first good run.

I took Dingo's watches on the bridge. The other qualified watchstanders were stretched thin enough as it was.

That's where I was one ship's night when Halley Keracides came to see me. "I thought you could use some company."

I let my skepticism show. "That's the only reason you're here in the middle of the night?"

"No." She sat down and stared at the displays for a long time. In jump space, they're mostly blank. Whatever's out there doesn't register. There'd been a time when I'd whiled away boring night watches thinking about what I'd do if something ever did show up on the displays while we were in jump. But nothing ever did, and there were a lot more likely to happen things to spend my time worrying about, and after a while I stopped thinking about it. Halley finally looked back at me. "We need to talk. About what happened to Third Officer Dingo."

I nodded, trying not to look angry or defensive. "Talking won't make it not have happened."

"Kilcannon, you know as well as I do that running a ship with systems this old and in need of repair is just asking for more accidents like the one that killed Dingo."

I kept my voice level, somehow. "It's been a real long time since anyone died on the *Lady*."

"I know. I checked. And, frankly, given the shape this ship is in that means you've been doing an incredible job." Halley paused while I tried to absorb what seemed to be an unexpected compliment. "But no human can beat the odds forever. Not when the odds keep getting longer. Skill and hard work and determination can keep a ship going for a long time even when she's only held together by spit and prayers, but sooner or later the saints get tired of staving off disaster and let the worst happen."

I waited to see if she'd say more but she seemed to waiting for me. "What do you suggest I do? This run should pay out well. Well enough to springboard us for an even better run. That'll pay for a refit. Not a great one, but good enough."

Halley leaned forward, searching my face for something. "Kilcannon, a ship's only got so much life in her. *Lady*'s old. You can't make her new again for any sum of money you're ever going to see running cargos on the fringes."

"She doesn't need to be new again."

"Okay, you can't make her *safe* again. Not really. Not for any sum of money you have any realistic chance of generating on cargo runs."

"One good run. That's all we really need."

"Do you really believe that, or are you trying to believe that?"

I ignored her question. "Then we'll fix *Lady* up and she'll keep taking care of us. That's what Captain Weskind always says. Take care of the ship and the ship will take care of you."

"Captain Weskind." Halley shook her head. "As far as I've been able to determine, she hasn't left her cabin since I came aboard."

"She's busy."

"Does she really know what shape the ship is in?"

I hesitated and I could tell Halley Keracides noticed. "She's been briefed. I brief her daily."

"I see." I couldn't tell from her tone of voice just what Halley Keracides saw. "Does she know her entire crew could die at any moment?"

"That's not true."

"Yes, it is, and you know it. Those engines are running on borrowed time, Kilcannon. This whole ship is. Sooner or later the engines will fail and you'll never come out of jump."

I pretended nonchalance and shrugged. "I hear Haven's pretty this time of year."

"Haven?" She obviously knew about Haven, the sailor's paradise, which wasn't something you could say about a lot of managers. "Is that where you believe ships go when they don't come out of jump?"

"They've got to go somewhere."

"No, they don't. Not according to the physics. And even if they did, they couldn't go to Haven because there's no such place."

I made another shrug even though I could tell they were annoying her. "It's a big universe."

"Not that big. One single place where every sailor would be happy? No such place could be real." Halley slammed her palm down onto the arm of her chair. "Dammit, Kilcannon, I can't believe this. Why won't the Captain talk to me? I've never seen her and none of the crew will talk to me about her."

"I told you. She's busy. You know a ship Captain's responsibilities."

"I know they allow a few minutes a day to leave her cabin and talk to people her ship has rescued." She fixed me with a demanding look. "The truth, Kilcannon. In the saints' names, what's wrong with Captain Weskind?"

"She's…" I looked away but something made me tell the truth for the first time in a long time. "Multi-polar degenerative cognitive disorder."

When I looked back, Halley's jaw had actually dropped in amazement. "Untreated?"

"Yes. No. I mean, we haven't been able to keep the right meds in stock." It wasn't something I got to talk about and now the words tumbled out of me. "The right meds could help her even now, maybe. I don't know. Probably not. But the right meds cost money. A lot of money. So did doctors authorized to prescribe them. Weskind spent the money on the *Lady*, instead. It wasn't enough, but it was more. That's what she said every time I suggested keeping her body on an even keel, and even I couldn't explain how she'd get refills for special meds in some of the ports we hit."

"By the saints, Kilcannon, someone with untreated multi-polar can't run a ship!"

"*Captain Weskind can.*"

She sat back, eyeing me with an expression I couldn't read. "You do realize you have a legal responsibility to report a captain who's incapacitated?"

"Captain Weskind is *not* incapacitated!" I realized I'd yelled and my face felt hot. Halley's non-expression hadn't changed, but I tried to speak more calmly. "She needs a little extra help. That's all. She's in command."

"I see," Halley answered again in a tone that conveyed nothing. "How long have you known Captain Weskind?"

I rubbed my face with both hands, feeling embarrassed. "Since Galpin Prime. The *Lady* was in port. I met Captain Weskind there. I was just a kid."

"Galpin Prime." Halley pondered the name. "Not exactly the finest planet in the known universe."

"It's a cesspit. It's where I grew up." I looked away again, fighting off memories. "No hope and no way out. Until I met Captain Weskind. She didn't have to spend a moment on me. Not *one*. But she noticed me. She offered me a job on the *Lady*."

"As First Officer?"

"As a deckhand. I worked my way up. All the way from the bottom. Captain Weskind believed in me."

"She didn't have multi-polar then?"

"No. At least, it hadn't manifested itself."

"So, you owe her..."

"Everything."

Halley nodded slowly. "Does she know her ship is running drugs?" I didn't say anything, taking refuge in silence for a moment. "Kilcannon, I can read cargo manifests and I know when they don't make sense. I know what's really in those cargo containers."

I grimaced. "Technically, we're not 'running drugs.'"

"Technically. All you've got is the precursors used to make the drugs. Do you think that's going to save your necks if you get inspected by peacekeepers?"

"I don't know."

She looked more exasperated than anyone I'd ever seen. "You're going into Fagin Star System with an illegal cargo. If any privateers try to jump you, which has a very good chance of happening, you won't be able to call for help because the peacekeepers will confiscate your ship once they check the cargo. Then they'd throw you in jail. At least the privateers might let you go if you take off in the lifeboat."

"Look, Halley, you know the *Lady* broadcasts her condition to anyone looking. The engine output, the energy readings, the shield fluctuations, anyone who sees her is going to know she's a tramp. And they'll leave her alone because a tramp isn't going to be carrying anything worth the trouble."

Her eyes reflected disbelief now. "That's your plan? To count on the poor condition of your ship to protect you?"

"We don't have any other choice." I clenched my fists, staring past her. "You said it. The *Lady*'s at the end of her rope. We need to make a decent profit on this haul. Enough to get a few repairs done. That's all we need. Just that one break. Saints forgive me, I'm not proud of this. But it's our only chance. The only chance left for the Lady and for her crew."

Halley regarded me, her face hard. "And for Captain Weskind. What happens to her if she loses this ship?"

"I…she won't."

"There are places that would take her."

"*It'd kill her.*" I calmed myself again. "The *Lady*'s her life. I'll do what I have to do to save her."

"*Anything* you have to?"

I sat silent again for a moment. "No. Only whatever Captain Weskind would approve of. Or…understand." I closed my eyes, not wanting to look at Halley for a moment. "We had offers to run weapons into Fagin, you know. They would've paid better than the cargo I took."

"But Captain Weskind wouldn't have understood running weapons into a place where people are slaughtering each other."

"No, she wouldn't." I opened my eyes and glared at Halley Keracides. "And she taught me there's some cargos you don't touch no matter what."

"She must have been…she must be a fine Captain."

"She is. Don't tell anyone what I told you about her."

"Captain Weskind? You forgot the magic word."

"Please."

"I promise." She stood up and stared at me. But Halley Keracides didn't say anything else and after a long moment she left the bridge to me and the blank displays.

* * *

"First Officer Kilcannon?" Able Spacer Siri stood there, still thin as a refugee but with her eyes clear. "I…I wanted to thank you." Her eyes shifted and she spoke with almost desperate haste. "The dust would've killed me. Sure as hell. I was halfway there. I knew my only chance was to get away, on a ship where I couldn't get any no matter what, but nobody'd take a duster. Except you. I got clear of it, thanks to you."

I shook my head. "I just needed another spacer, Siri. Thank Captain Weskind. She's the one who gave you a chance."

Siri's eyes shifted again. "Uh, yeah."

"I'll let the Captain know you're grateful and you're clean."

"Uh, thanks."

* * *

We finally broke out into normal space, high above the plane of Fagin system, looking down on a small area of space where human rationality had been in very short supply for too long. As Lady dove down toward the fourth planet in the system we listened to news reports and shook our heads over the latest atrocities.

Two inhabited worlds and a slew of lesser bodies with colonies on them left too much territory for the peacekeeper forces to cover. Watching the news reports, it quickly became clear that whenever the peacekeepers scrambled to halt an outbreak of fighting in one area the people in the places they'd left would immediately start raising hell. From our perspective, that was good. It meant the peacekeepers wouldn't have any leisure time to wander about and investigate the small freighter coming in outside their normal patrol areas.

But everything wasn't great. From our position above the plane of Fagin's system, we could easily see all the ships operating below us closer to the plane. Two of them, one good-sized and one a bit smaller, showed up as freighters but were loitering not far from the area we'd pass through enroute the fourth planet.

"Privateers?" Halley asked me.

"Yeah. Sure to be. You know as well as I do that freighters hang around ports, waiting to off-load or on-load. They don't hang around the middle of nothing."

"Even with freighter engines they wouldn't have trouble intercepting us. What are you going to do, Kilcannon?"

"Keep going, cross my fingers, and hope they either ignore us as not worth the trouble or something else happens to distract them."

Halley Keracides just nodded and watched the read-outs for a while with me.

There's a reason the old saying warns to be careful what you wish for. Less than a day later we were watching news reports of the latest mass slaughter by the good people of Fagin system. There was (or rather, had been) a colony on a moon of the fourth planet which was (or rather, had been) inhabited by a group most of the people on the fourth planet didn't like for some reason. The peacekeepers protecting it had been drawn away and the fourth planet people had struck.

"Saints, what the hell's the matter with them?" Chen asked, not bothering to hide his revulsion.

"I don't think there're any saints watching this system," Halley Keracides answered.

I was watching something else. "There's a ship heading out our way." They followed my mark. "Looks to be an old freighter. A lot bigger than *Lady*, but a bit older, I think, from the readings we're getting."

Within another six hours we'd seen news reports confirming that the old freighter had come off of the moon where the colony had been wiped out. Nearly wiped out, that is. They'd gotten most of their kids and some of the adults onto that freighter. Its path to the peacekeepers or other safety in-system blocked by hostiles, the freighter had hauled mass out of the plane of the system in the hopes of getting away.

Our two loitering privateers started heading for it. They'd been well-positioned for an intercept and they'd catch the fleeing freighter. No question. About two days before the nearest peace-keeper ship could possibly arrive to protect the freighter. And just a few hours before we swept safely past on our way to that fourth planet.

"You've got your distraction, Kilcannon," Halley Keracides stated in a very quiet voice.

"Go to hell."

"What are you going to do?"

"There's nothing we can do. *Lady* doesn't carry weapons. She's old, she's tired and we can't do a damn thing."

Halley nodded, but she didn't seem to be agreeing. "Maybe you ought to brief Captain Weskind."

If I'd spotted even a trace of mockery on her face or in her voice I'd have sealed her in her quarters until we hit port, but there wasn't any of that. "I should," I agreed, and left to do that.

Captain Weskind sat and listened. She always sat while I talked, and after I'd finished I waited. But Captain Weskind didn't recite her hopes about 'one good run.' She just sat there, her face flickering with rapid shifts in emotion, and after a while I excused myself and went back to the bridge, wondering if Captain Weskind had taken a turn for the worse, or if she could no longer say whatever else she might've wanted to say.

The two things nightmares have in common with space is that you can fall and never reach bottom, and everything happens in slow motion. The old freighter was running for all it was worth but the privateers were closing fairly easily, and because of the distances involved it was all taking days to play out. Yet I could read the end without any trouble. I'd been driving ships a long time and could handle relative motion by instinct. I didn't even need to consult the maneuvering systems to know about where the privateers would catch the freighter.

Since the freighter had come out of the area of the fourth planet, the same area we were headed, and had run in our general direction, the privateers would catch it pretty damn close, as space goes, to where Lady would pass. They'd be busy killing the kids and looting the ship, of course, so they wouldn't spare a glance at us.

We'd just have to watch it happening.

And Halley Keracides watched me. She didn't say any more, she just watched me and the read-outs, where as the hours spun down prey ran and predators chased and the *Lady* got ever closer to both.

There's always points of decision when you're driving a ship. Given your mass and your engines you can tell how long you have to make up your mind before it's too late to be able to do something. We were six hours from the place where the pursuit would end. Halley Keracides and I were the only ones on the bridge of the *Lady*. She stayed silent, but we were coming up on that point of decision soon and I finally had to say something. "Just one good run."

Halley Keracides nodded. "And one more after that?"

"Yeah. That's all *Lady* needs, right?"

"No. Not really. But you've got a clear shot at it."

"At the fourth planet, you mean."

"Yes. If that's what counts."

I kept my eyes on the displays. "And after we deliver our cargo we'll have to find something in Fagin system that people will pay to have delivered to another system."

"The people you deliver that stuff to will have something they want you to haul. Count on it. Whether you want to haul it is another question."

"This is an honest ship. I swear."

"Today, I'll agree with you. Tomorrow, maybe not. What course do you want to steer, Kilcannon?"

"I know what course I won't steer. But…damn. One or two runs…we could get them done and then drop that crap for legit cargo again."

"Is that what you think?"

"I don't know."

"What's Captain Weskind think?"

I didn't want to hear that question. But Halley Keracides looked and sounded sincere when she asked it, and I knew it was a question I ought to know the answer to. "I'll brief her on our options."

"So now you think you have options?"

"For a little while longer, yeah."

Captain Weskind wasn't awake but this was a critical time, and any Captain knows they'll be awakened when necessity calls. I talked to her, laying out the situation again. I discussed options, I made a recommendation. I waited.

Captain Weskind sat there. Not a word, and too many changes coming too fast in her facial expressions for me to even try to read meaning. Feeling an ache inside, I prompted her. "This could be a good run. The one we've been waiting for."

But she didn't respond. And I knew I had my answer. Captain Weskind had given me that answer a long time ago, when I was new to the *Lady* and she was teaching me the ropes. Small players in the freighter trade sometimes had to take a flexible approach to rules and regulations. But she always told me there were some cargos you didn't take on, some things you didn't do. And some things you didn't let happen if you could do anything about it.

Halley Keracides was still on the bridge. She looked a question at me, but said nothing. I did some calculations, then I adjusted our course a bit, sat back and waited.

"You're going to come a lot closer to those privateers," Halley observed.

"Yeah." I called engineering. "Vox, I want you to rig the autos so they can best handle all engine functions, even emergency damage."

"Can't."

I muttered a prayer to any saints watching. "You need to do your best."

"Already did."

"In a few hours I'm going to have you evacuate engineering and stand-by at -."

"No."

"Dammit, Vox, what's the problem?"

"Saw the course change. Know what you're gonna do. Go help them kids. Gonna need us here. We're staying."

For the Chief Engineer that amounted to a very lengthy speech. "Okay. But when I say you have to go I want you guys out of there as fast as possible. Understand?"

"Aye."

Halley was watching me again. "What?" I demanded.

"Just wondering what you're planning and what I can do."

"I'm planning on using the two weapons available to the *Lady*."

Her eyebrows rose. "I didn't know you had even one weapon on the *Lady*."

"People are clever, Ms. Keracides. We can turn all kinds of things into weapons. As for you, I'm going to have you and the others from the *Canopus* suit up and stand-by at the lifeboat."

"Chen will insist on staying in engineering with your people."

"Fine, the other five of you will go the lifeboat."

"Why are we going to need the lifeboat? You're not planning on putting us off while you somehow go into battle, are you?"

I took a deep breath. "No. We're all going to need that lifeboat."

Word spread through the crew. I waited for a mutiny that didn't happen. I told everyone to suit up. Once the privateers figured out that *Lady* might be a threat they'd open fire. It wouldn't take many hits by them for *Lady* to lose atmosphere.

I left Halley Keracides on the bridge for a few minutes while I went back to Captain Weskind's cabin and got her into her own suit, then pressurized it. "I'll be back, Captain. Just wait for me and don't worry."

Halley was in her suit by the time I got back. The Vestral Company suit she wore looked new or very close to it. I couldn't help comparing it to the suit I had on, which in its patches and worn fittings betrayed every hour of too much use over too many years. But if Halley Keracides noticed the differences between our suits she didn't show it.

One hour out. I called for more thrust from *Lady*'s engines, and the old girl started putting on more speed. That called for another adjustment to our course. Down and off to the side we could see the privateers closing on the big freighter. So far they hadn't paid any apparent attention to us. I tried to match a freighter-turned-privateer mentality to my own experiences and wondered how long it'd be before they started worrying that *Lady* was more than just a tramp freighter trying to sneak past them.

By adding speed I'd set us up to intercept the privateers a bit earlier, at a point a little further from the big freighter than before. I didn't want to risk them shooting up the freighter any before I got there.

"Why haven't they opened fire on the freighter already?" Halley asked.

I made a sour smile. "You wouldn't understand, I guess. When you think of spare parts you think of going to a shop and buying them new. Ships like the *Lady* live on what we can salvage. I know what they're thinking. They don't want to damage stuff on that ship. They're going to overhaul that freighter, put in a few well-aimed shots at close range to knock out his ability to maneuver, then board, space the kids and strip everything off the freighter that they can use or sell."

"Why not just keep the freighter?"

"It's too easy to track stolen ships. It's hard to track stolen parts." Halley at least had the grace not to remind me that I'd already demonstrated my knowledge of the illicit parts market.

An alarm pulsed and I watched the read-outs tell me a chunk of metal had just raced past us. "I guess that was a warning shot."

Halley nodded. "They're using rail-guns."

"Sure. The electromagnets are easy to build and maintain. And the metal blocks they use for ammo are cheap and really easy to manufacture. Just the thing for a bunch of people who want to keep shooting at each other for a long time."

"What are you going to do about the warning shot?"

"Ignore it. By the time they figure out I'm ignoring it we'll be a lot closer."

"You're going to get a whole lot closer, aren't you, Kilcannon?"

So she'd guessed what I intended doing. "Yeah. I can't act too soon, though. I have to wait as long as possible or they'll be able to get up enough relative speed to dodge us." I checked the distance and the time. Not much than another half-hour. "I want you to get down to the lifeboat now. You, the others from the *Canopus*, and the rest of *Lady*'s crew. Get into the lifeboat and standby."

"How sure are you that the lifeboat isn't going to be hit when they start shooting at the *Lady*?"

Not sure enough. "The lifeboat is out on one side of the ship, and the privateers will be aiming at Lady's center to maximize their chances of a hit. The lifeboat should be okay even if the privateers really shoot us up while we're closing on them."

Halley eyed me. "Tell me you're not going to ride *Lady* all the way in."

The thought brought a shiver up from somewhere deep inside me. "Hell, no. But it'll be close. It has to be. I need everyone else at the lifeboat waiting."

"Alright. The saints know you've promised to try and make the lifeboat, Kilcannon. You don't want to meet them with a broken promise fresh on your record. Remember that. For my part, I'll keep that lifeboat waiting as long as I can." She hesitated. "Should I get Captain Weskind?"

"No! She won't go with anyone but me. I'll bring her with me."

Halley Keracides looked like she wanted to argue, but then nodded and left. About ten minutes later she called the bridge and reported that everybody was at the lifeboat. Everybody but the guys in engineering, Captain Weskind and me.

A moment later another metal projectile whipped by *Lady*. I wondered how long they'd give me to react this time. But it hadn't been a warning shot. More projectiles came in, aimed straight at *Lady*. I heard and felt the impacts, grateful that the storage spaces in the bow were taking the brunt of the first volley. That's why they were there, to absorb damage if *Lady* hit something or something hit *Lady*.

But storage spaces aren't armor and those metal projectiles were fast and heavy. There was a pause of a few minutes after the first volley, apparently to see if we'd take the hint after actually being hit, then more rounds started coming in. This time they started punching through. Tiny hurricanes roared through Lady as the shots from the privateers ripped holes in her. Atmosphere vented from a score of holes in the hull, pushing Lady slightly off course as they did so. I corrected the course and watched the instruments report dropping air pressure until every compartment in the ship was in vacuum.

I checked the read-outs again, watching the paths the other ships made as they swung through space, and I knew it was time. I brought *Lady* around, finally steadying her pointed at the spot where the smaller privateer would be in fifteen minutes. The barrage of projectiles halted for a moment as my course change avoided shots aimed at the place where Lady hadn't gone. In the momentary calm, I popped a console I'd never opened in earnest and threw two switches.

On the outside of the hull, massive grapples opened and electromagnetic pushers engaged as the emergency cargo jettison system activated for the first and last time on *Lady*. The big cargo containers which ringed the ship at two places were pushed away from *Lady*, slowly spreading out around the course she was on. As the last containers cleared the hull I goosed *Lady*'s engines to the maximum we could manage. The old girl shook and shuddered, but she accelerated away from the containers, leaving them traveling behind us down the same course. As I turned *Lady* slightly again, I watched as the delayed commands I'd fed to the cargo containers activated and they started offloading drums of precursor chemicals through load points located on their tops and bottoms, the drums drifting into the areas between and among the big cargo containers. Good riddance to a cargo I never should've loaded.

In the process of clearing my conscience I'd also created a huge shotgun blast aimed for the point the smaller privateer would reach in twelve minutes. I wondered how long it would take the privateer to spot what I'd done, figure out what it meant and try to alter its trajectory. It shouldn't matter. Freighters, even freighters fitted out as privateers, weren't designed to dodge wide debris fields aimed right at them.

I steadied *Lady* just short of a collision course with the larger privateer. The longer I could leave that privateer thinking I was only planning a close firing run, the better.

Ten minutes. "Vox, evacuate engineering *now*."

"This is Chen. Vox is dead. We took some hits back here and suffered power arcs."

Damn. "The rest of you get out of there and get to the lifeboat."

"How much longer -."

"Go!"

"Aye, aye. On our way."

Lady's hull twitched and rang with impacts as kinetic rounds from the privateers hit again and again. I sat there, watching compartments and systems report damage or just go dead as the solid metal chunks tore into and through *Lady*. I wondered what would happen if a round came through the bridge. Would I have time to realize it or would I just find myself face to face with Dingo, him demanding to know what I'd screwed up this time? Eight minutes. Close enough and maybe too close.

I made a small course correction, finally fixing Lady onto a collision course, then I locked the docking system onto the big privateer and deleted the engine braking and maneuvering overstress limitation sequences. *Lady* would steer herself directly at the privateer, engines going full blast, as long as her systems still functioned. I stood up, fighting for balance as *Lady* jerked to maintain her lock on the big privateer, and stared at the screen where the shape of privateer loomed. Then I ran for the Captain's cabin.

Captain Weskind was there. Face down on her desk. She'd opened her suit. There wasn't any time to see how long it'd been open and how badly she'd decompressed. I sealed the suit and repressurized it and sat her limp body on the edge of her desk and turned my back to her and draped both her arms forward over my shoulders and grabbed her hands and lifted her on my back and ran for the hatch.

I staggered down passageways which swung wildly as impacts and sharp maneuvers to keep the ship aimed at the privateer altered *Lady*'s motion. The lights flickered, caught, then finally died, leaving dim patches where the few working emergency lights came to life. What must have been a metal projectile from one of the privateers burst through a bulkhead three meters in front of me and went corkscrewing on, chewing another hole through *Lady*'s guts.

Ten meters from the lifeboat access the deck suddenly bent and rose on one side, then the bulkhead slapped me. I hit the other bulkhead, my vision graying out, then managed to get to my feet again, Captain Weskind still a dead weight on my back. Something inside *Lady* screamed as it tore under stress, the sounds transmitted through her structure and into my suit. She was dying. Saints forgive me she was dying. I stumbled down the weirdly narrowed passageway to the junction, then one more meter to where outstretched arms waited.

Captain Weskind was pulled from my back and then I was pulled in as well, the lifeboat hatch being slammed shut almost on my feet. I felt the hard deck beneath my back and remembered the lifeboat was overcrowded. People were screaming but my head was swimming too much to understand. Then a great hand pressed on me as the lifeboat accelerated away from what was left of *Lady*, putting everything it had into getting away. I struggled to breathe as a couple of bodies lying partly across me tripled in weight.

A black fringe grew around my vision as I lay there, but I kept my eyes fixed on the display screens at the front of the lifeboat. The one in front of the piloting station showed only the spinning star field, but the auxiliary screen was locked on the area where *Lady* was still heading.

The big privateer was accelerating, trying to get up speed, finally realizing Lady was playing for keeps, but its own mass and inertia were holding it back. *Lady* came down on it, moving so much faster under her long acceleration that the old freighter seemed like an arrow. The privateer was still firing, but the shots were only chipping pieces off *Lady*. They couldn't stop or divert her.

Lady roared down from above like the angel of death and struck across the privateer at an angle. I fought back the blackness and what might have been tears as *Lady*'s old hull bent around the point of contact. The privateer's hull bent, too, curving upward on either side of the impact. I could see hulls shredding, compartments blowing open under the stress and spilling their contents into space, countless minor detonations rippling through the merged wreckage as systems and structures failed explosively. A cloud of vented gases blocked direct view of the wrecks as they spun off, locked together in their death throes.

Off to the side, the slower-moving cargo containers and cargo drums were coming down on the smaller privateer. It was moving, too, trying to dodge the field of debris. It almost made it. Drums hit, denting the hull or punching through, but the smaller privateer managed to hold its course. Then a big container clipped its bow. The privateer shuddered and lurched off to one side under the impact, directly into the path of another container. The second one hit aft and hit hard. I watched energy flare and knew the privateer's engines had slagged. The smaller privateer staggered into an erratic roll, taking more glancing impacts as it spun away.

I couldn't see the refugee ship. I couldn't remember where it was supposed to be relative to us now. I tried to find it but my head hurt and I felt very tired and it was too hard to keep that blackness out of my eyes, so I let it fill my eyes and my head and let the pain go away.

* * *

I opened my eyes and saw light again. Smooth light, steady light. I blinked, turning my head to see what looked like a very well-appointed sick bay. I turned my head the other way and saw Halley.

She nodded at me wordlessly, waiting for me to speak.

"This doesn't look like a peacekeeper prison infirmary."

Halley twisted her mouth into a sardonic smile. "No. The peacekeepers figured they owed you one. You're on the Vestral ship *Fenris Rising*. Outbound from Fagin."

"Oh." I thought about that. "*Lady…*"

"The collision totally destroyed the larger privateer. The smaller was knocked completely out of commission by the impacts of the cargo containers. The peacekeepers rounded it up a few days later."

"A few days later." I lay back, feeling a lot more tired than someone who'd been asleep for at least that long ought to feel.

"Peacekeepers picked us up. Good thing. That lifeboat of yours wasn't in very good shape. Neither were you. Concussion, a few broken bones. That kind of thing. The refugee ship made it, by the way. They're safe."

So *Lady*'s sacrifice hadn't been in vain. I nodded.

"Captain Weskind would be very proud of you, Kilcannon."

"Captain Weskind -." The question stalled as I saw the look on Halley's face.

"She's dead." Whatever Halley saw in my expression made her lean forward a bit and squeeze my hand. "You did everything you could. Her suit must've been open at some point. Yes? She'd suffered too much decompression. You got her onto the lifeboat, but it was too late."

I was silent for a long time, letting the sorrow roll through me. And the guilt of relief. Captain Weskind had died on the ship she loved. Maybe she'd understood enough of what was happening to make that decision. Now she'd no longer have to face a universe her mind couldn't deal with anymore. Now she wouldn't have to try to go on without the *Lady*. But when everything else had passed, one thought still stung. "I think I remember her being pulled on the lifeboat before me."

"That's right."

"The Captain should've been the last one to leave the ship."

Halley leaned back again and regarded me. "The *Lady*'s Captain was the last to leave the ship."

"You just told me you took Captain Weskind onto the lifeboat first."

"So I did." I waited, but she didn't explain her statement. "Any more questions?"

"Yeah. Who the hell are you?"

Halley gave me that twisted smile again. "I have a confession to make, Kilcannon. Keracides isn't my real name. My actual name is Halley Vestral."

"Vestral?" The name took a minute to connect. "As in Vestral Shipping?"

"Yes. My mother's the majority owner."

I inhaled deeply. "I wondered why First Officer Chen deferred to you. As if you weren't just some passenger."

"He knew who I was and so did the Captain of the *Canopus*. Nobody else on the ship did. Mother and I often travel under false names for security reasons."

"Good thing, I guess. Why tell me now?"

"Because I want to offer you a job, Kilcannon. After consulting with the Vestral Shipping officers and sailors who observed you on the *Lady*, my mother agreed without reservations."

A job. With Vestral Shipping. On a bright, clean ship. "That's…
thank you. I, uh, know I'll need to work my way up from whatever
I'm hired at -."

"The job offer is for Captain of one of our ships."

I just stared for a long moment. "I'm not qualified."

"We think you are."

"I've never served as a Captain."

Halley started to speak, then paused. Eventually, she just nodded.
"We think you're qualified," she repeated.

"What about the rest of the crew from the *Lady*?"

"I knew you'd ask about them. We'll find positions for all of
them." Halley paused again. "That System Tech. Siri. Some people
were panicking while we waited for you in the lifeboat, trying to
get us to go. She kept her body across the lifeboat hatch so no one
could close it until you got there. She's awful strong for such a small
girl."

"I'll have to thank her, if I ever see her again."

"You will. She's signed on as crew on this ship." She saw my face.
"She's clean now and deserves the opportunity. It's the least I could
do, Kilcannon."

"Uh, thanks." The word felt so hopelessly inadequate, but what
could I say that would convey what the offer to me meant? I wouldn't
be roaming the docks, trying to find another old ship willing to hire
me on as, maybe, Third Officer. Instead, I'd be Captain of one of the
bright, shining ships of Vestral. With a full crew and a maintenance
budget. Good runs to good planets.

I ought to feel something.

I leaned back against the bed, wondering why everything seemed
so empty. Here was everything I'd ever dreamed of, everything I'd
ever envied, everything I'd ever wished for. I had it. "Why aren't I
happy?"

I hadn't realized I'd spoken that until Halley shook her head. Her
eyes were looking right into mine, as if she could see something

there. "I'm sorry. You aren't happy because you know the odds are vanishingly small that you'll ever find Haven again."

"Haven? What are you talking about? I've never found Haven."

She smiled that not-a-smile again and shook her head once more. "You still don't know where Haven is?"

"I've never known where Haven is. And I thought you said Haven isn't real."

"No, I said there isn't any *one* place which *all* sailors could call Haven. But it does exist."

Riddles. I couldn't handle them at the moment and broke eye contact with her, staring up at the overhead. "Then where is it?"

"Kilcannon, you fool. Haven is that place you most want to be, the place that holds everything important to you."

When I looked down again she was walking away. I wondered what she'd meant.

Saints, I miss the *Lady*.

AUTHOR'S NOTE
AS YOU KNOW, BOB

Reviews are often the bane of writers. This is especially true if the reviewer chooses to write about the book they wish the writer had written rather than the one the writer did write. Sometimes the reviewers' complaints leave writers scratching their heads in bewilderment. And sometimes that all works out fine. When the first book in my Lost Fleet series was published, one reviewer took *Dauntless* to task for many perceived sins. Among these were assertions that it wasn't multi-cultural enough, and didn't contain explicit references to trendy new science fiction concepts, and above all didn't explain in detail how everything worked. In short, I was being called to task for not having done the sort of things for which SF is often mocked by the wider world. The reviewer concluded that *Dauntless* could have appeared in John W. Campbell's old *Astounding* magazine. As it turned out, many readers yearned for that sort of story, so the put-down ended up generating a lot of sales for me. In addition, the review inspired *As You Know, Bob*. I got a lot of good things out of that negative review.

AS YOU KNOW, BOB

The agent: How's that science fiction novel you've been working on coming along? Send me an excerpt from the beginning so we can see about getting it into shape for today's market.

* * *

The story begins: The phone rang with Bob's signature tune, so Bill tapped the receive button. Bob's face appeared, looking unusually enthusiastic since he normally tried to coast through life with minimum effort. "Did you hear about the frozen Lumpia?"

"Not yet." Lumpia. That sounded important enough for Bill to pause his work and face the phone. "As you know, Bob, frozen Lumpia isn't nearly as good as fresh."

"This stuff is! There's a new process. Meet me in the lobby and we'll go get some and check it out."

Bill's conscience tugged at him. "I dunno, there's this analysis of the signals from the Eridani Probe that I'm supposed to be running . . ."

"It'll be there when we get back."

"Okay." Bill stood up, powering down his workpad and heading for the door.

In the hallway he met Jane, a researcher who worked a few doors down. Bill tried not to stare as she crossed her arms and looked at him. "You're in a rush. Going on some important mission?" she asked dryly.

"I guess you could say that. I'm going to pick up some frozen

Lumpia." Bill hesitated. Jane had the kind of smarts and attitude that had always attracted him, but she had never shown much interest in Bill and had turned him down the one time he had asked for a date. Maybe she would be willing to consider a more casual errand together. "Do you want to come along?"

Jane pulled out a money card and checked it, then shrugged. "Sure. Why not? I need to pick up some stuff, too."

* * *

The agent: This is okay, but I can't sell it. Something's missing. It's not SciFi enough, do you know what I mean? This is supposed to be happening in the early twenty-second century and there's nothing about the singularity or nanotech or quantum states or cyberspace or posthumans or multiculturalism or complex antiheroes. How can you call that SciFi? I know, I know, you've told me that when people use tools they don't think about how they work. But readers expect certain things from SciFi. Oh, and the characters. Those aren't SciFi characters. Punch them up and make them the sort of characters you see in *real* science fiction. And get some gratuitous sexual content in there.

* * *

The revised story begins: The singularity had crashed and burned in a viral-cataclysm that had destroyed most of civilization and every decent coffee house east of Seattle. Now a complex array of probability states undulated down a fiber-optic line surviving from pre-singularity days. The electrons carrying the message didn't so much move as they did alter the places where they had the highest probability of existing.

Since the electrons didn't truly exist anywhere, neither did the strange cyber-world in which they didn't move, filtering through an immense alternate reality in which normal physical rules of the macro-world didn't apply.

Entering a complex series of transformational states, the electrons that weren't there interacted with the receiver mechanism, propagating through layered nano-light-emitting-diode projectors to generate a three dimensional image.

A tune distinct to the originator of the message chimed from the nano-manufactured receiver. It was the First Movement of Genghis Juan Feinstein's folk-rock Hindustani opera, which, William knew, meant the message had to be from Roberto Sigma, the latest in a string of complicated and untrustworthy clone/cyborg hybrids who nonetheless followed their own indecipherable code of honor. William moved his palm over a light sensitive but robust section of his desk to command his virtual work-station to pause in its operations. Now as the stacked image displays created a perfect visual representation of Roberto Sigma, William saw that the enigmatic posthuman seemed happy about something.

"I assume," Roberto Sigma began in the Libyan-Croatian accent he had acquired from his last neural-upgrade, "that you are aware of recent developments in micro-cryogenics."

William nodded, his own implants from his days as a special forces commando during the Betelgeuse incursion activating automatically at the sight of his sometime friend/sometime enemy. "As you know, Roberto, cryogenics hasn't yet worked to expectations, especially since several promising lines of research were lost when the singularity crashed."

"Ancient history, William! That is so five nanoseconds ago. I know of a means to demonstrate how well the new process works. It originated in Asia. Interested in meeting me to investigate it?"

William hesitated, his implants jangling internal warnings. The last time he had followed Roberto Sigma it had been into an unending maze in cyberspace from which he had narrowly escaped. But if what Roberto was saying was true, he had to know. "I've been working on analyzing signals from the Eridani Probe. It's been using the new quantum state transmitter to tunnel data through to us at amazing speed."

"If the signals have propagated through quantum paths they will still have a probability of existence when you return."

"You're right. I'd forgotten about the addendums Jonquil made to the Hernandez postulates back in 2075," William agreed. He gestured another command over the light sensitive control pad, ordering his workstation to shut down and watching as it swiftly cycled through functions and closed them before powering off automatically.

William stood, his lean muscles rippling as the commando implants amplified William's own natural speed and strength. There weren't a lot of former special forces commandos doing astrophysics research, so he tended to stand out during the virtual conferences. William walked across the floor tiled with panels from the Toltec/Mayan revival period, nano-circuits in the panels sensing his movement and sending commands to the door, which slid open silently on nano-lubricated rails as William approached.

He slipped cautiously into the hallway and saw Janice from a few pods down, the nanoparticles in her lip gloss making it glow a delicious ruby red. Janice spun to face him with all of the pantherish grace you'd expect from a first degree black belt, her blue eyes watching William speculatively. He tried not to stare back. At 23 years old, Janice was the most brilliant and the most beautiful quantum physics researcher in the entire world. What was left of the world after the singularity crash, that is.

Janice crossed her arms, drawing William's gaze to the magnificent breasts which led her hetero-male colleagues to speak admiringly of the amplitude of Janice's wave functions. "You're in a rush. Going on some important mission?" Janice purred.

"You might say there's a high probability of that," William replied. "I need to acquire some samples of a new cryogenic process."

Janice's gorgeous eyes narrowed. "Are you talking about the

Renz/Injira process? I understand that freezes organic matter in crystalline matrices that preserve cell structure. When it's returned to normative temperature its composition is perfectly preserved."

"That's what they say. I need to find out if it's true, and there's a certain item of Asian origin which will give me the answer." William hesitated, feeling a strong attraction to Janice that had nothing to do with the gluons holding her quarks into such an attractive package. She had once told him that they would never occupy the same space. Did her exclusion principle still apply to him? "Would you like to come along?"

Janice's eyes glowed a little brighter as her nano-vision enhancement implants reacted to her excitement. She reached into one pocket and checked the charge on the twenty-gauss energy pistol she carried everywhere. "Sure. I'd calculated there was a high probability of deflection in my plans for today. It looks like I was right."

* * *

The agent: Much better! Very SciFi. But I did notice that the story doesn't seem to flow as well as it used to. Maybe you can fix that by using some of the real cutting-edge concepts. You know, quantum foam and dark energy and stuff. And try to make the characters a little more exotic. You know. Weird. More science-fictiony. Give it a shot and see if you can clean the story up a bit.

* * *

The re-revised story begins: Wilyam sensed the arrival of a message from his old rival and comrade Robertyne, who had existed in an indeterminate state since an accident while researching applications in the mysterious world of the quantum foam, where literally anything was possible. Waving a hand to freeze his work in mid-motion above his desk, Wilyam waved again to bring up the message display.

Particle functions coalesced into a functional framework

emitting radiation on visual frequencies. The familiar features of Robertyne appeared as if he/she were actually looking at him through a window, though Wilyam suspected that Robertyne had actually ceased to exist some time before and he was really speaking directly to the inexplicable presence that seemed to animate the quantum foam. The image of Robertyne displayed a very human smile, though even when Robertyne had been unquestionably posthuman he/she had never been easy to understand or to trust. "Have you heard the ripples in the foam, Wilyam? Organic matter from the macro-place you call Asia now exists in a frozen state without flaw."

Wilyam frowned as the implant linking him to the bare edges of the foam glittered with possible outcomes. He saw himself in a million different mirrors, each one reacting slightly differently to Robertyne's proposal. "As you know, Robertyne, nothing actually exists, so it isn't possible to preserve something that doesn't exist. Previous attempts have produced probability chains that wander off into reduced states of replication quality."

"There's something new/old/past/present/future in this perception reference, Wilyam. It represents a low probability outcome of extreme accuracy."

It sounded tempting to the millions of different Wilyams staring at him from the could-be's dancing around the implant. "I'm busy analyzing signals from the Eridani probe. We're not sure if they're from our probe or if signals are tunneling from an alternate probe in another reality."

"Then split your probabilities and attend to both and neither. I am everywhere and nowhere, but will center a probability node below here."

"Okay." Wilyam focused on the implant, drawing on the strange properties of the quantum foam to create infinite possibilities. He waved a hand to shut down his work and stood up/remained sitting and continued working.

The door's probability state cycled as one Wilyam approached, going to zero for an instant as that Wilyam walked through.

In the endless hallway beyond, Jandyce from a few stationary states down floated with her eyes closed. She opened them, her eyes glowing blue from the tap implanted in her brain which connected Jandyce directly to the dark energy which filled the universe. Wilyam tried not to stare, knowing Jandyce was tied into cosmic currents none of his probabilities could hope to grasp.

She crossed her arms, drawing Wilyam's observations to the two symmetrical anomalies superpositioned on her chest, both far exceeding functional limits in a way that excited his ground state and also provided proof that dark energy could overcome the pull of gravity. "You're in a rush. Going on some important mission?" Jandyce hadn't spoken, but her voice echoed in his head.

"The foam has found something new. A way to preserve matter in an hitherto unknown way. There's a sample from the human-reality matrix of Asia." Wilyam hesitated as his millions of selves around the quantum foam link swirled in every possible action-outcome sequence. Jandyce and he usually demonstrated weak interaction. When he had once asked her about the possibility of mutual reinforcement, she had informed him that the likelihood of direct reactions between quantum foam and dark energy was infinitesimally small and shown him the Feynman diagram that proved it. But he had long hoped for a probability sequence that could result in entanglement with her. Perhaps, somehow, their wave/particle dualities could constructively interfere in a way that would generate mutually beneficial patterns. "Would you like to come along?"

Jandyce's eyes glowed brighter as the dark energy flowed. Matter swirled as she reached beside her and plucked a patch of darkness from nothing, examining it closely. "The cat lives. I will go, maintaining the proper balance of forces and perceptions."

* * *

The agent: Great! This I can sell. It's pure SciFi. Nobody could understand what's happening or why these, uh, people are doing whatever it is they're doing. Tell you what, though, it's still a little rough. I mean, how do you explain what's going on? Readers want to know how this stuff works. So how about you polish it a little, provide some explanations, and give me one more look, okay? Oh, and put the sex back in. You didn't take it out? Well, then, make the sex *understandable* again. Make the sex so *anybody* can understand it. Heck, make the whole thing so anybody can understand it.

* * *

The re-re-revised story begins: The great wizard Wil sensed a message from his companion and challenger the Baron of Basi. He waved one palm and the magical mirror on a nearby wall glowed, showing the image of the Baron, who gave Wil a searching look. "Have you heard? From far in the east, that which we have long sought can now be ours. It lies frozen."

"Frozen?" The Wizard Wil gestured again and the fires blazing beneath his cauldron sank to a low glow. "As you know, Baron of Basi, nothing once living survives well being encased in ice."

"The Grand Council has found a way, I tell you! A way we must investigate before the Bane of Dargoth does! That which we desire lies frozen in a state of perfection. Come down from your tower and we shall seek it together."

"A quest?" The Wizard Wil turned a doubtful look on his cauldron. "I have been seeking to interpret certain messages from the stars."

"Surely a wizard of your powers can deal with two tasks at once."

"There is a way," the Wizard Wil agreed. Calling up the proper spell in his mind, Wil summoned an elemental assistant and ordered it to continue his work. He walked toward the door, the earth spirit bound to it seeing his approach and opening the portal, then closing it behind him.

Outside stood the Sorceress Jainere, who sometimes appeared in the south tower of Wil's fortress. Jainere, her eyes glowing with the fires of the powers that lay beneath the world humans knew, sought wisdom in places few dared venture. Now Wil tried not to stare at the beauty she barely concealed behind a few filmy garments, her breasts glowing with a magic older than time that offered the promise of pleasures no man could withstand. The sorceress Jainere crossed her arms under those breasts, smiling enticingly as she saw the reaction Wil could not hide. "You're in a rush. Going on some important mission?" she inquired in a voice that rang like the tiny bells the dancers of Dasiree wore.

"We seek that which was frozen and can be rendered perfect again once thawed," Wil spoke haltingly despite his efforts to resist the spell of Jainere. "It comes from the lands far to the East, where priests and priestesses with skins the hue of the sun have long guarded it." He had desired Jainere for many lives of normal men, but the unpredictable sorceress had always scorned him, declaring that no sorceress could live by the rules of right and wrong which Wil followed. Perhaps if she joined the quest Jainere would finally learn enough about him to desire uniting their powers and their lives. "Do you want to come along?"

Jainere reached down to the slim, bejeweled girdle which hung on her hips in a way that made men's minds go astray, drawing forth the enchanted mirror in which she viewed images of what might be. "Your possible futures are of interest. I will accompany you. It might be amusing."

* * *

The agent: Now that's more like it. Fantasy! There's a big market for that now. It's a lot easier for readers to understand than SciFi and people seem to be able to relate better to the characters.

I wonder why they don't want to read science fiction as much these days?

AUTHOR'S NOTE
DO NO HARM

This story had a simple premise. If spaceships (or anything else) is built with a capacity to detect damage and self-repair, you are essentially giving it an immune system. That is a good thing, as a rule, but immune systems don't always work as they're supposed to. In fact, they often go off kilter. The ship that can repair itself might find itself suffering a form of auto-immune disease. When that happens, what kind of specialist is going to figure out what is wrong and how to fix it?

DO NO HARM

"Sandra's acting weird, the geeks can't figure out why, and the boss is spinning like a pulsar."

Kevlin pulled his attention out from the immersive medical simulation long enough to give Yasmina a questioning look. "I thought Sandra was supposed to leave this morning."

"Right. She won't go. Come on. The director's called an all principals meeting."

"I'm a doctor," Kevlin objected. "I'm supposed to keep the people working for the corporation on this station healthy. Why do I care about Sandra's problems?"

Yasmina smiled back at him in a mocking way. "I'm a doctor, too. If I have to go, so do you."

"They need you to analyze the project director's mind just in case he gets really dangerous this time," Kevlin suggested. "I'm just a simple country doctor with a low-gravity, space illness specialty."

"Sure. Then you'll come in handy if the director bursts a vein while he's yelling at everyone." Yasmina beckoned. "Come on."

Grumbling just loud enough for her to hear, Kevlin paused the sim and followed her down the hallway. "I could always monitor the director's health from my office," he suggested.

"Nice try. Didn't your teachers at med school ever tell you not to try to con a shrink?"

Sandra was still at loading dock four alpha. Yasmina led the way onboard the ship, then along a passageway that ended in Sandra's control room. The limited area was already full of exasperated engineers of various types and persuasions, some looking dejected, some angry and some staring into space as they tried to think. "Why can't we do a virtual meeting?" one complained as Kevlin and Yasmina wedged their way in.

Another engineer answered in an accusing voice. "Because the director found out you guys had been hacking the meeting code so you could have avatars sitting in for you while you did other stuff. Now we all have to crowd in here in person so he can be sure we're all actually getting yelled at."

"People have been hacking virtual meeting code since the stone age," the first engineer protested, then hastily stopped speaking as a short man with a lofty attitude and an ugly frown strode in, the crowd somehow contracting away from him so he had free room.

"Report," the director stated, glowering at the chief designer.

The chief designer, who had been arguing with Sandra's captain, made a helpless gesture. "Sandra won't work. Something's shorting out her central control functions."

The director's glower deepened. "The Spaceship Autonomous Network Developmental Research Application is the most expensive project in the history of this company. I expect more from you than vague reports that it just doesn't work! Are you saying the control network isn't receiving the commands?"

"No," the chief designer responded in a tight voice. "I'm saying that the control network isn't responding to external signals. It's in some kind of weird loop, with only a few apparently random signals going out to minor sub-systems. We give a command and nothing happens."

"Nothing happens? Something has to happen! If nothing is happening that means something is happening!"

Kevlin gave a glance at Yasmina, who was watching the director with a fascinated expression. He just knew she would love to get the director into a controlled environment so she could analyze his mental processes.

One of the other engineers tapped the air in front of him, activating a virtual display. "This is what Sandra's central processing activity is like."

Yasmina looked suddenly startled as an image appeared overhead. "That looks like an EEG of an epileptic seizure."

Eyes swung to focus on the doctor. "An epileptic seizure?" the director asked in a deceptively mild voice.

Though it was obvious she regretted speaking, Kevlin wasn't surprised that Yasmina refused to back down. "Yes," she insisted. "That's what that looks like. If I saw that representation of signal activity in a human, I'd say it was a seizure."

"This is a ship," the designer protested.

"Yes," Yasmina agreed. "A ship you constantly refer to as if it were human, as if it were alive, talking about the complexity of an internal and external sensing network that mimics that of a living creature. I've read the specs on the central command system. You modeled it on basic brain functions. Well, maybe that means it's subject to the sort of problems living brains develop."

Kevlin waited for an outburst of laughter or scorn, but it didn't come. A third engineer nodded with a wondering expression. "The operating system is incredibly complex, full of learning routines and development loops. It could've developed problems like that."

"How do we cure it?" the director demanded. "In people?"

This time Yasmina grimaced in the way of a doctor trying to explain complex things in lay-person's terms. "Short term, we use medications that raise the seizure threshold. Long term, we go in and fix whatever is causing the brain to short-circuit."

The chief designer's eyes narrowed in thought. "Short-circuit? What could have caused that happen? Sandra's central command functions were working fine yesterday. We haven't modified them since then."

"Stray signals?" another engineer suggested.

"The central command area is shielded."

"Maybe some other part of the, uh, neural network on Sandra?" Yasmina offered.

This time everyone's attention turned toward a senior engineer, who looked defensive. "The test monitoring equipment couldn't –"

"It's wireless!" the director snapped.

Sandra's captain and the chief designer were studying something. "Stray signals. That would do it. They must be filtering in through the sensing network. Oh, hell. I bet they're reflecting down these access trunks and into the command circuit sub-junctions."

The director's glower deepened as he barked another order at the hapless senior engineer. "Turn it off!"

The senior engineer punched some commands into his personal, and a moment later the depiction of Sandra's control system activity cleared. A muted cheer sounded, choked off as the director stabbed a finger at Sandra's captain. "We've already lost two hours. Get this thing underway and get the tests done. Everybody else who isn't part of the crew get off this ship now!"

Yasmina turned to go, but stopped when the director called out again. "Not you, Dr. Finshal. In light of the fact that we needed your assistance to correct this problem with Sandra," he added with a scowl at the chief designer, "I think it would be wise if you go along on the test voyage.

"I hope you enjoy the trip," Kevlin whispered, taking a step away.

"Dr. Shan!" Kevlin barely avoided wincing as he turned to face the director. "You, too. Since one type of doctor was able to diagnose a problem with Sandra, having a physician along too might be a good idea."

"Um, but I need to –"

The director had already vanished down the passageway. Most of the engineers vanished in his wake, leaving only the ten members of Sandra's crew and the two doctors.

* * *

"This is all your fault," Kevlin grumbled to Yasmina. They were strapped into acceleration seats at the back of Sandra's main control room.

"Think of it as an adventure if that helps you cope," she replied.

"An adventure? We're just going outside Lunar orbit and coming back. Some adventure." Kevlin 'tapped' the virtual screen before his seat, bringing up different images, pausing briefly when he reached one showing an outside view of Sandra still docked to the station, Earth's globe floating serenely in the background. Someone had positioned that shot with the skill of a public relations expert capturing an important moment. Finally he settled on the crew status display, providing real-time updates on important activity within the crew's bodies. "Some of the crew members were up all night," he observed out loud.

"Really?" Yasmina frowned. "I've recommended against that sort of thing."

"They've been doped. Looks like pentastamine. Yup. As good as a full night's sleep."

"I don't care," Yasmina grumbled. "There's no substitute for natural sleep."

Kevlin shrugged. "The stuff's been tested –"

"I know! I also know there's a lot we still don't understand. The human body and brain are incredibly complex."

His reply was cut off when the captain raised her voice. "Sandra. Separate from the station and proceed along preplanned track Alpha One."

A cool female voice replied. "Command understood. Complying."

Yasmina's scowl deepened. "I told them to have her repeat back the command so they could be sure she actually had heard them right. But they complained that was inefficient since they know everything about Sandra and how she'll respond. You'd think their experience this morning would have suggested they don't know everything about her."

"Her?" Kevlin asked. "You're talking about Sandra as if she's alive, too."

"So? Look." She reached across and brought up a different display for him. "This monitors all systems. What does that look like?"

Before him, an image of Sandra loomed, the ghostly exterior allowing a clear view of representations of sub-systems depicted with visual cues for performance. The power system's branches pulsed green, the filaments of the command network glowed golden throughout the ship, life support flared blue. "I hadn't seen this before," Kevlin admitted. "It does look like a living thing. Is that just how the display works?"

"Not entirely. The ship integrates the latest tech using living models. There's a host of macro and nano-based devices swarming through the hull to keep all sub-systems working right and in repair. It's all networked under the central control system, linked into one entity." Yasmina shrugged. "I've got a subspecialty in psychocybernetics so I was involved in some of the design discussions. Not that Sandra has consciousness or can develop it. But her functions run along lines suggested by things like the human brain stem."

Kevlin saw commands racing through the depiction of Sandra's 'nervous system,' then the ship lurched as it detached from the station, pushing clear of the rotating structure and swinging around. The main drive cut in and slammed him against the back of his seat. A black fringe wavered around the edge of his vision as the acceleration grew.

"Sandra!" The captain called in a voice tortured by pressure. "Keep ship's movement within crew comfort parameters."

"Command understood. Complying." Sandra's voice, of course, wasn't stressed at all.

The acceleration slacked off. Kevlin took a grateful breath and shook his head carefully. "Why did she have to be reminded of that?"

Yasmina was watching the crew in the command seats arguing

among themselves. "I imagine that question is being debated right now."

After that, very little happened of interest to Kevlin. Sandra bored a hole through empty space on a trajectory avoiding normal space traffic, while the engineers put her through various tests. Kevlin monitored the crew's physical states, spotting the reactions that told him when Sandra had performed particularly well and the other reactions that indicated something Sandra had done had generated concern. That got old, too, until on a whim he brought back up the display showing Sandra's inner workings and compared it to the human crew's as the ship went through her paces.

"What's so fascinating?" Yasmina asked.

Kevlin blinked at her, taking a moment to refocus. "I was just watching the behavior of the ship's sub-systems. If I didn't know better, I'd think I was seeing autonomous physical reactions."

"I told you it was modeled on that."

"No, I don't just mean actions in response to commands. It looks like reactions to the commands, to how well the ship performs. See?"

Yasmina peered across, her face intent. "That's weird. I haven't seen that reported. No, wait. There's been some reports of transient system behaviors. The geeks thought they were caused by learning routines and would damp out as the system matured. Are you seeing that?"

"No. They're getting stronger and more obvious." Kevlin took a look at the crew, who seemed calm enough, then checked their physical states. Stress was obvious there in a lot of cases. Something was bothering them. "Has Sandra failed any tests so far?"

"Not as far as I can tell. Results keep showing her exceeding expectations."

Sandra's voice sounded again. "Cooling sub-system module seven suffering from degraded performance."

Kevlin focused on that component, seeing the images marking

nano and macro scale automated maintenance drones hastening to the site. Nothing seemed to happen for a while as the devices clustered on the ailing component, then a second wave of repair drones appeared, bulling past the first wave. Within moments, the module's performance markers improved. "Did Sandra just create a new repair capability?"

One of the crew heard him. "We call it evolving. The system learns what new capabilities are needed and modifies existing equipment."

"Where does it get the resources? Does it cannibalize existing equipment?"

"It can." The engineer grinned and highlighted a display showing the first wave of now-obsolete repair drones being disassembled by some of their successors. "There's also a small supply stockpile onboard for her to draw on during the test voyage. We didn't top her off since we didn't know how she'd work until we put her through her paces."

"Good," Kevlin muttered. He saw Yasmina eyeing him.

"What's bothering you?" she asked.

"Nothing."

"Right. And I can't judge thoughts from exterior cues. What's wrong?"

He frowned, not wanting to admit it. "Evolves. I don't like that."

"There's limits. Sandra can't evolve into sentience."

"They're sure?"

Yasmina nodded. "I was in on that design work. Sandra's control system is roughly analogous to the more primitive parts of the human mind, the stuff that handles basic functions. There's nothing that can evolve into a higher brain function because the space is tightly constrained and the resources are fenced off. In order to modify itself enough to achieve a simulation of sentience, Sandra would have to be sentient to begin with."

"You're telling me she's just operating on instinct?"

"Pretty much."

Kevlin tried to relax his frown. "So all we have to worry about is instinctive level behavior. I hope they didn't forget about the id."

"Oh, no!" Yasmina declared in a dramatic voice. "They forgot about the id!" She chuckled. "It's been ages since I've seen that ancient video but I still remember that line. The id doesn't really exist, you know."

"Something does that we can call the id," Kevlin replied.

"Sandra doesn't have ancestral behavior patterns inherited from a long line of evolution," Yasmina noted sharply.

Kevlin subsided, gazing morosely at the displays again.

* * *

They watched, they ate the boxed meals provided, they watched some more. The crew made things happen, made things go wrong, made things break, and watched Sandra take corrective action. As minor incidents were properly handled and Sandra's abilities evolved, the tests continually got harder, stressing the ship's responses. Most of the action was apparent only on the displays, though, as events unspooled inside the ship away from the control room.

Kevlin switched displays restlessly, even taking a while to watch the view from the chase ship which was following Sandra as a safety precaution. But watching a ship whose motion wasn't apparent against an unchanging backdrop was like staring at a painting. A little of that went a long way. Kevlin finally dozed off, waking to see it was late at night on the human clock, though of course the star studded darkness outside Sandra hadn't changed.

Voices were raised in the forward part of the control room. The argument there was probably what had awakened him. The captain noticed Kevlin was awake and directed a question his way. "What do you think of this?"

Kevlin's virtual display lit with an image of Sandra. He studied it, baffled as to why the crew would be asking his opinion about anything to do with the ship, then spotted a section about two-thirds of the way back on the ship. Something had bulged out into the passageway there, pushing into adjacent areas as well and even cutting off a couple of sub-system circuits. Frowning, Kevlin zoomed in the display, seeing that the mass consisted of hundreds of identical components, fused together. "What's going on?"

"We have no idea," the captain barked. "Sandra doesn't seem to understand it and claims she can't stop it. Our best guess is that one of the repair segments locked somehow and keeps replicating the same component."

"Out of control replication?" Kevlin couldn't hide his reaction. "Like a cancer?"

"Cancer?" The captain looked baffled, then appalled.

One of the other engineers nodded quickly. "Her repair systems have been evolving rapidly under the pressure of the tests. One of them must have evolved in a way that bypasses Sandra's control functions."

"How do we stop it?" the captain demanded.

"Uh." Kevlin scratched his head, noticing that Yasmina had also woken up and was watching them with a captivated expression. The woman got her kicks out of the strangest things. "Starve it? Can you kill power to it? Or prevent whatever's building the components out of control from getting access to more resources?"

The crew members went into a huddle. The captain called out several orders to Sandra, looking steadily more unhappy as each command failed to choke off the equipment tumor still growing into the passageway. Finally she turned to two of the crewmembers. "Chen and Ragosa. You two go down there and manually cut through these circuits and feeders. See? I'm downloading the diagram to your personals. The repair drones can operate without external power for a limited period but then they'll shut down in that area. That'll at least stop that thing from growing any more while we identify the bad components." She frowned again as the two unbuckled and floated free of their seats. "Take your suits."

"Ah, hell," Chen protested. "We'll be carrying enough as it is with the laser cutters and manual tools."

"Wear your suits! I won't get nailed for violating safety precautions on a shakedown voyage!"

Kevlin watched them go, then gazed at the display again.

"Now what?" Yasmina asked softly.

"I don't know. Something is nagging at me. I can't figure out what it is."

"Do you think those two are in danger?"

"No." Kevlin shook his head. "I don't think so. How could they be? There's safeguards built into the system, right?"

"Sandra's full of them," Yasmina agreed. "She can't try to harm people, or let people come to harm. You're still worried about something serious going wrong?"

"They've mimicked the operation of a living organism, Yaz. Unpredictable and living go together."

"How could it bypass the safeguards?"

"I don't know!" Kevlin made a frustrated gesture. "They designed this thing's internal functions, especially its self-operating and repair functions, to 'evolve.' What are the limits on that?"

"I told you. Sandra can't get sentient."

Kevlin glowered at his display. "There's a whole lot of things that go wrong in living organisms that operate below the level of sentience."

She frowned at him, but said nothing more, apparently thinking.

* * *

Chen and Ragosa reached what even the crew had begun calling a cancer and started cutting.

"Alert," Sandra's voice declared dispassionately. "Interior damage in port aft main passageway between frames sixty-five and sixty-six."

"Acknowledged," the captain replied. "Authorized repair work is underway."

A moment passed, then Sandra spoke again. "Alert. Interior damage in port aft main passageway between frames sixty-five and sixty-six continues and is intensifying."

"Acknowledged," the captain repeated. "This is authorized repair work."

"The ship is suffering internal damage," Sandra repeated, her voice somehow sounding insistent to Kevlin.

The captain frowned and went into another huddle with the other engineers, only to be interrupted by a call from Chen. "Hey, what's Sandra doing? There's all sorts of repair drones showing up and milling around. Ah, damn. Some of them are repairing the cuts we're making!"

"Sandra!" the captain shouted without waiting to reply to Chen over the circuit. "Cease repair activity in port main passageway."

"Command understood. Complying."

Chen came back on, sounding aggrieved. "Why aren't you telling Sandra to stop?"

One of the crew spoke up. "Here it is. Sandra's acting on our commands but doing almost immediate resets in response to the stimuli from her internal damage sensing network."

For some reason, the captain swung and gave Kevlin an accusing stare. "Can you explain that?"

Kevlin swallowed before answering. "If Sandra were human, I'd say it was like telling someone not to scratch when they keep feeling an itch. Just how closely do your damage and repair network feeds to the central control system resemble the stimulus-response process to discomfort or pain in a living creature?"

"Sandra doesn't feel pain," someone insisted.

"She feels something that prompts her to action, doesn't she?"

The captain gave his crew another glance, then they began talking rapidly again in low voices that didn't carry well.

Yasmina spoke to Kevlin in a whisper. "Are you wondering at what point a stimulus-response system evolves into a pain network?"

"Yeah. They can say it's not pain, but if it triggers the same defensive response in the organism, then what's the difference?"

Sandra spoke again, her voice definitely more urgent. "Damage spreading in port aft main passageway. Require immediate response."

"Hey!" Chen roared over the communications circuit. "We're being swarmed by those damned drones! They're fixing the cuts faster than we can make them!"

"Go to full power on the laser cutters," the captain ordered him. "Get those cuts done fast so Sandra will calm down."

Silence fell for a moment as the engineers in the control room tapped rapidly through screens. "Making good progress now," Chen reported. "The cutter is frying some of the repair drones that get in the way, though."

"Damage spreading rapidly in port aft main passageway!" Sandra sounded very urgent now. "Immediate action required."

"Sandra, repairs are underway," the captain repeated in a frustrated tone. "Take no action."

Kevlin felt something, and glanced back to see that the hatch leading onto the bridge had opened. No one was there waiting to enter, though.

One of the crew noticed, too. "Sandra, reseal the hatch to the bridge."

"Command understood. Complying," Sandra replied, her voice its usual dead calm again.

The hatch didn't close. "Sandra, reseal the hatch to the bridge," the captain ordered this time.

"Command understood. Complying."

"Captain?" Another engineer was staring at something on his display. "She's doing instant resets again after acknowledging our orders. Every interior hatch and door on the ship is open."

The captain stared at him, then spoke in a powerful voice. "Sandra. Close all doors. Command override Sigma Sigma Sigma."

"Command understood. Complying."

"It's not closing," Yasmina observed.

"Damn!" one of the crew exclaimed. "We had to give Sandra a reset capability so she could function autonomously, but she's started using that to get around our commands."

"She's not using it," Yasmina objected. "There's no conscious thought involved. I'm sure it must be a defensive response operating below the level of consciousness. Her subsystems are telling her something has to be done so she's working around obstacles to action."

"Captain! Airlock doors are opening! Interior and exterior!"

The captain hesitated the barest fraction of a second before yelling and springing into action. "Into suits! Everyone into your suits and seal them! Chen! Ragosa! Seal your suits!"

The emergency suits were stored next to the seats, fortunately. Kevlin's hands were shaking as he pulled on the suit, fumbling with fittings that should have been second nature after countless emergency drills on the station. A growing breeze was tugging at him as he struggled to get the chest seal in place.

"Strap in!" the captain was shouting. "As soon as you get the suit on, strap in and then get your helmet sealed!"

Kevlin dropped into his seat and pulled the harness across, clicking it into place just as the breeze grew to a gale of wind trying to suck him out through the hatch and ultimately out through the airlock. Wondering if he was really gasping for air already, Kevlin got the helmet down, trying not to panic as the suit automatically pressurized. Cool air flowed from the recirc unit and Kevlin slowly got his trembling under control. Shocked by a sudden realization, he looked over and saw Yasmina also strapped in, her own suit just finishing pressurizing. Ashamed that he had forgotten about her, forgotten about anything but his own fears, Kevlin looked away again.

"It's okay," he heard Yasmina over the suit's circuit. "Perfectly natural reaction."

Kevlin mumbled a reply, wishing she hadn't been able to understand his embarrassment.

Other voices came over the circuit, the captain's finally overriding them all. "I need an estimate as to why that happened. Anybody? Any ideas?"

It suddenly seemed so obvious. "Sandra is trying to get rid of us," Kevlin stated.

Momentary silence followed that declaration, then the captain came on again in a deathly calm voice. "Explain that. There's numerous safeguards built into the operating system that puts human safety at a premium. Sandra can't attack humans."

"She's not attacking humans," Kevlin explained, feeling more and more certain. "Her repair sub-system is attacking an infection. Don't you see what you've been doing? You've been deliberately causing damage to her, on an escalating level. Her repair system has dealt with it at every stage, evolving the whole time. Well, it's a simple leap from being reactive to the damage to reacting to what's causing the damage. The cutting back there was the last straw. To Sandra's repair system, we're parasites at best and harmful infections at the worst. Sandra can't override the actions of her repair system any more than we can without the help of targeted medications."

"She tried to expel the parasites?" the captain asked. "What happens if that doesn't work?"

"I'd imagine her repair system will go after the parasites directly. Her repair system is rapidly developing an immune component. I should have seen that coming. It's a logical progression for any such system."

The captain's voice rang through the circuit. "Chen! Ragosa! Stop cutting and get back here!"

"But we're almost through –"

"Stop cutting! We can see a new wave of repair drones headed your way! Get out of there fast!"

The wait for the two engineers to return seemed interminable. Chen and Ragosa were pulling themselves through the hatch when it started closing. They barely cleared it before it sealed. "We've lost all internal control," someone reported in a desperate voice.

Kevlin saw the captain gazing around as if thinking through her next action. "Alright," the captain announced. "I'm declaring an emergency. All nonessential personnel are to leave the ship. Get to the boat and stand off in it. We've lost comms to the chase ship, so bring them up to date."

The captain and three other crew members remained seated, but six of the engineers unstrapped and began hauling themselves to the hatch, beckoning to Kevlin and Yasmina to follow them. Kevlin unstrapped as well, making a point of waiting until Yasmina had done the same and started after the engineers. Scared as he was, he wouldn't race ahead of her.

Two of the engineers had braced themselves and were tugging at something. The hatch swung open reluctantly under the pressure of the emergency release.

The journey through the ship to the boat dock was strange. The passageway was deserted, yet to Kevlin it felt haunted. He couldn't look at a bulkhead without thinking of Sandra's pseudo-life functions pulsing behind them.

The engineers reached the access panel to the boat dock and wrestled its manual control until that opened reluctantly as well. The first one who started to enter the dock stopped and stared. "It's gone."

Kevlin shifted so he could just see over the engineer's shoulder. The boat which should have filled the dock simply wasn't there even though the outer hatch remained sealed. On the deck, a swarm of repair drones were picking at a diminishing pile of something.

One of the engineers laughed in a slightly hysterical way. "I was wondering where Sandra was getting the resources to build so much. She ate the boat."

"Oh, God," another engineer responded. He tried calling the captain, to no avail. "Back to the control room. Let's go before those things try to recycle us."

The captain gave them a startled glance when they returned, her face setting into grim lines as her engineers reported what they had seen. "That does it. I'm pulling Sandra's plug. Once she's off, we'll get aft and shut down the main power supply." Unstrapping, the captain went to the aft bulkhead and lifted a cover to expose a large manual switch.

Kevlin gave Yasmina a questioning glance as the captain pulled the switch down. All of the lights went out and Kevlin's virtual display vanished, leaving only the lights on the suits to illuminate the control room.

"The Frankenstein switch," Yasmina answered Kevlin's unspoken question. "Some people also call it the wooden stake or the silver bullet. Every artificial intelligence system has one built in that manually cuts all power. Just in case the AI starts singing 'A Bicycle Built for Two.'"

"How many artificial intelligence systems have built in autonomous repair capability that can operate without power for a while?" Kevlin asked.

The captain heard, stared toward Kevlin, then placed one palm over the bulkhead next to the manual cut-off switch. "I can feel activity behind the bulkhead."

"They've identified the cause of Sandra's problem." The lights came back on. "And they've fixed it. Captain, you've got a wonderfully effective simulation of a living organism here in terms of identifying injuries and taking corrective action. And it knows what keeps trying to hurt it, and that we just tried to shut down its brain."

"Sandra can't be sentient!"

"She's not! It's all happening at a level way below sentience!"

Kevlin yelled. "Why should that be a surprise? Out of all the threats to human life, how many are sentient and how many are essentially mindless like bacteria?"

A momentary silence fell. "Can we stop the drones if they try to take us out?" someone wondered.

"What about the nanos? Sandra's sub-systems have been modifying them right and left. The rate of evolution seems to be on a exponential curve."

"If it's like the evolution of living organisms, most of the modifications will be harmful or useless and die out," Kevlin suggested. "Some of them might even threaten Sandra."

"Most will die out? Or some might further harm the ship? That's not all that reassuring, doctor. The seals on our suits are supposed to keep out nanos, but nothing's perfect." The captain gestured. "We're abandoning ship. Everybody out. Back to the boat dock."

Repair drones of various kinds were visible in the passageways this time as they pulled themselves through the ship. Kevlin stared as he saw several drones attack another and disable it. They had to veer to one side as a bulkhead bulged perilously toward them. In another area, drones were busy dismantling what Kevlin recognized as a cooling unit. "She needs that!" one of the crew protested. "Why would Sandra take apart an essential component?"

"Sandra isn't," Kevlin insisted. "Her sub-systems are doing it. Just like when humans run short of calcium and the body robs it from bones to keep the teeth strong. Part of the repair sub-system thinks some other part of Sandra needs those components more."

The last remnants of the boat had vanished along with the drones which had digested it for Sandra. The captain and another engineer tugged at the emergency release on the outer hatch with no results. "I'll have to blow it using the explosive bolts." She yanked open a panel, pulled out a battery, connected leads to two attachments behind another panel, then pushed a button.

Faint echoes of the explosions reached Kevlin through his handhold on the ship as the hatch swung out. The captain turned to face them. "Push yourselves clear of the ship. We don't dare wait here for rescue from the chase ship. Go!"

They went. Kevlin shoved off, looking back to see Sandra's shape diminishing behind him, the captain's suited figure going last out of the hatch. He heard her calling the chase ship on the distress frequency. "SOS. We need emergency pick up. Full macro and nano-scale decontamination required. Remain clear of Sandra. Repeat, remain clear of Sandra."

Kevlin wondered how long the recirc unit would keep him alive. Full scale decontamination took a while. But then, he couldn't argue with the captain's order, either.

* * *

Yasmina joined him at the display, looking like she'd been vigorously scrubbed with sandpaper over every part of her body, every hair shaved clean. Kevlin knew he looked the same, and knew she also felt like her insides had been similarly sandpapered. He would probably shudder for the rest of his life whenever someone mentioned a full macro and nano decontamination.

She gestured at the image of Sandra. "What's happening? Any guesses?" Sandra's clean lines had been distorted by random bulges. Remote readouts showed system failures cascading through the ship.

"She's dying," Kevlin stated. "Pure and simple. Some of her repair functions evolved into harmful out-of-control infections. Other parts of her are attacking her. See this stuff? Any immune system risks getting too efficient. At that point it starts attacking itself. You can see where all the control system filaments in this part of Sandra are dead. I'll bet her own repair system is destroying them."

"Auto-immune diseases," Yasmina observed in a shocked voice.

"Yeah. The testing process matched with learning routines and an ability to improve repair capabilities inevitably pushed Sandra into becoming better and better at identifying and fixing damage. Unfortunately, living organisms are obvious lessons that there's no optimum point at which that stuff stops. It keeps trying to get better even after it gets so good at its job that it turns harmful."

The captain had come to stand with them, her face sober. "It shouldn't have happened. We knew everything there is to know about every one of the components on that ship."

Another engineer shook his shaved head. "It's a scientific principle that you can know everything there is to know about something, and still not be able to predict an outcome. We just proved it again."

"Assuming you did know everything," Kevlin snapped. "You tried to make a machine work like a living creature, with self-direction and self-repair capabilities. What made you think you could tell how it would act? Humans are the mature result of millions of years of evolution and we only function halfway well because of an enormous investment in cultural, organizational and medical systems designed to control our actions and compensate for our faults!"

"What'll happen to Sandra?" Yasmina wondered.

The captain glanced at Kevlin. "Do you think she'll be safe once the power dies and everything goes dark?"

"The macro stuff, probably. I don't know about the nanos. It all depends if they evolved in the direction of viruses that can remain dormant for almost indefinite periods while awaiting conditions to reactivate."

This time the captain grimaced. "We'll have to junk her. There's no telling how some of her internal components have evolved, so we'll probably use an automated drone to show her onto a trajectory into the sun. We'll have to severely limit or block evolution of nanos on the next model. Maybe not even use them. They're too hard to track if they do start changing. But we can put limits on the macro drones, too. We'll do better next time," the captain vowed.

"That statement probably could've been carved on a substantial number of tombstones throughout human history."

"Next time will be different," the captain insisted.

"You're right about that," Kevlin agreed. "Next time I won't be aboard."

"Yes, you will."

"No, I won't. My contract clearly limits the duties to which I can be assigned."

The captain smiled. "If you're right, these ships will need medical expertise to identify, diagnose and treat problems. One of the potential duties listed in your contract is ship's doctor. So congratulations. That's what you'll be. The ship's doctor."

AUTHOR'S NOTE
DOWN THE RABBIT HOLE

One of the good things about attending conventions (and there are many good things) is that I get exposed to information that can help generate new stories. At one convention in Baltimore, I heard Dr. Catherine Asaro giving a talk about the latest research into hyper-velocity space travel and what physics currently told us regarding things like faster-than-light. One thing struck me after that talk. Our nervous system works at the speed of light. How well does it work if we're moving faster than that? Years before I had read about how the human mind tricks us into thinking that we see things that we don't. And then there's that trick that dancers use to keep from falling over with dizziness when they're spinning around over and over again. On top of that, Stan Schmidt the editor of Analog, had challenged me to come up with a reason why pilots of aircraft might not make the best spacecraft pilots. Put them all together, and there's a story in there.

DOWN THE RABBIT HOLE

"We'd like you to pilot the next Prometheus probe, Commander Horton."

Commander Josh Horton fidgeted slightly despite the padding in his chair, his eyes darting around the conference room, resting for the briefest moment on the face of one NASA administrator before leaping to the next. Every face held the same forced cheerfulness, the same projection of an honor conferred, and the same more-or-less poorly hidden anxiety. "The next Prometheus probe?" he finally asked. "I didn't know there'd been a first."

"Well, you understand security, Commander, don't you? A successful test of a faster-than-light propulsion system would have incalculable significance for the human race. We certainly don't want to generate false hopes prior to a successful test."

"So the first probe wasn't successful?"

Administrator eyes shifted helplessly for a moment, then steadied. "No. At least, we don't think so. There's been no contact with any of the probes since they engaged their FTL devices -"

"*Any* of the *probes?*" Horton demanded. "There's been more than one failure?" Silence met his question. "Look, people, I deserve to know what's going on before you strap me into that can."

"Yes." The senior-most administrator nodded his head ruefully. "You do deserve that. There have been six Prometheus probes launched. None have returned. We have no idea why."

"Six?" Commander Horton's brain hazed momentarily, then he shook his head several times to clear it. "What, they blew up?"

"No!" The woman who'd answered looked around, embarrassed by her outburst, then repeated her reply firmly. "No. The only energy discharge noted was that predicted from the FTL transition. No other discharge. No debris. No events noted downrange."

"Downrange." Horton ran the word around his mouth for a moment. "Downrange can be measured in light-years, right? If something blew up when it came out of FTL you wouldn't see it for years, maybe."

"That's correct. However, sufficient time has elapsed so that we should have been able to observe such events from the tests by now."

"I see." Horton licked his lips, closed his eyes, then nodded. "Well, I guess we've got to keep trying." Then his eyes shot open and he looked around the table again. "Wait a minute. You said you wanted me to pilot the probe. But I'm a Systems Officer, not a pilot."

"Yes, Commander. We know that. That's why we're asking you to, uh, occupy the probe for this test."

* * *

Earth's sunlit arc, splashed blue/white/brown, hung within Josh Horton's line of sight. Next to the small viewport stood Dr. Orasa, waiting patiently for Horton's attention to return to her. "Sorry, Doc," Josh apologized. "I've never been up here on the station before. The views are pretty impressive."

"That they are," Dr. Orasa agreed. "Seeing the Earth from here always reminds me of that scene in the movie where the waltz is playing as the space station rotates majestically. Of course, our station doesn't rotate. Do you remember that scene?"

"Oh, sure. Everybody involved the space program knows that one. But that's not the movie I was thinking of just now."

"Really? Some other space epic?"

"Uh uh." Josh smiled in half-embarrassment. "I was thinking about the old musicals. You know, with the spectacular dance routines."

"Yes…" Dr. Orasa replied with a mix of puzzlement and patience. "I always loved those routines. Watching Gene Kelly and Fred Astaire and Ginger Rogers and Ann Miller dance like you figured angels would if angels ever acted in films with silly plots. So, I was looking out and thinking what kind of dance routines those people could have done up here in zero gravity. Imagine it!"

Dr. Orasa smiled in reaction to Horton's enthusiasm. "I suppose I can. Be that as it may, Commander Horton, I'm sorry my information won't be as dazzling. In truth, there's very little I can tell you."

"I thought you were a hot-shot quantum physicist, Doc."

"I am," she replied with another slight smile. "The problem is that just about everything we know about conditions on the other side of the light-speed barrier is theory. All I can do is summarize that theory for you."

Horton nodded somberly. "Because nobody who's actually been there has made it back."

Anguish shadowed her face. "I'm afraid that's correct. We don't know how moving faster than the speed of light will affect many things. Our nervous systems, for example. Or your perceptions of everything around you. Do you understand the concept of a frame of reference?"

"Yeah." Josh nodded again. "The Three Stooges did a routine about that once."

"The Three Stooges?" Dr. Osara blinked in evident confusion. "They did a routine about alternate frames of reference?"

"Yeah," Josh repeated. "In the skit they were carpenters, I think, and Moe and Larry got into an argument over which way was Right and which was Left. So Moe calls over Curly and tells him and Larry to stand facing each other, then tells them both to point to their Right. Well, naturally Curly points one way and Larry points the exact opposite way, and Moe gets mad, calls them knuckleheads and slams their heads together. But they were both pointing the right way, based on their own frames of reference. Right?"

Dr. Osara blinked again. "Uh, yes. That's…roughly the concept involved. You'll be perceiving the Universe in a manner different from any of us who aren't traveling at your velocity."

"But you don't know just what that'll mean."

"No." She managed another smile. "I hope you won't consider me a knucklehead because of that."

Josh smiled back, trying to ignore the tight knot which persisted in forming in his guts. "Nah. You don't know what you don't know, do you?"

"Uh…no. Good luck, Commander Horton."

"Thanks. One more question, though. Do you know why I specifically was picked for this mission?"

Dr. Orasa shook her head, frowning slightly. "No. I can't imagine it was because of your fondness for Ann Miller and the Three Stooges, but I don't know what criteria were used for your selection."

Half an hour and fifty meters later, Josh stood staring at the object which held his fate. Prometheus Seven, resembling nothing so much as an outsized round trash can with a slightly convex nose, sat locked within its cradle inside the space station's service hanger. Slight bulges around the probe's surface marked coverings for instruments and communication systems. Josh Horton ran one gloved hand along the titanium alloy skin of the probe, as if he could somehow feel the metal through the layers of his spacesuit, then levered himself into the cockpit where ranks of gauges and displays grown familiar in brief but intensive training now stared back at him. "Nobody ever told me why this thing is streamlined," he complained.

Colonel Linda Gutierrez smiled briefly. "No one knows what kind of resistance exists in the FTL environment. It's purely a safety precaution, just in case turbulence associated with the FTL transition, or resistance on the other side, might be able to harm anything sticking out."

"Like my neck, you mean?" Josh muttered. "Is that also why there isn't any porthole?"

"That's right. That, and, um..."

"And?" Josh asked sharply.

Colonel Gutierrez grimaced but nodded in acquiescence. "Since you've met with Dr. Orasa you know we have no concept of how things will look in an FTL environment. The outside view may be profoundly disturbing. By using viewscreens you'll be able to shut off that view if you need to."

"If the viewscreens work. I mean, the lenses are electro-optics, and Dr. Orasa pointed out I'll be moving faster than their signals. Heaven only knows what I'll see. Or what I'll think of it." Josh rubbed the back of his neck, frowning in thought. "Now what does that remind me of? Seeing and moving fast and thinking. Oh, yeah. A long time ago I saw some show on the way humans see things. You ever hear about that?"

Gutierrez shrugged. "Maybe. There's a lot of interesting things about the way human systems work."

"You said it. Well, this one talked about how when you're spinning you see things rushing past in a blur. Only it turns out you don't."

"You don't?"

"No. They found out the optic system can't process something it sees that's going by that fast, so what your brain really sees when you sweep your eyes past something is a blank spot. But the brain can't handle blank spots, so it generates a picture of what it thinks should be seen, only the picture's blurry because the brain can't remember all the details. Cool, huh?"

"Unusual," Colonel Gutierrez agreed. "But, regardless, on this flight you shouldn't need to see where you're going, Commander Horton. After the FTL drive kicks in you do a straight run for ten minutes, then a timer drops you back into normal state. If calculations are accurate, that should place you about twenty light minutes downrange when you depart the FTL state."

Horton's mouth worked as if he were tasting something unpleasant. "And if somewhere along that way there's some real big rock in my way? What do I do if I can't see it coming?"

Gutierrez shook her head, face solemn. "Commander, at the velocity you'll be traveling you wouldn't have the chance of a snowball in hell of turning quickly enough to avoid an obstacle."

"Great," Josh grumbled. "This is like putting on a blindfold and diving into a pool without knowing if there's any water below. I guess if I do hit something you'll see the fireworks."

"We haven't seen any fireworks in the prior tests," Gutierrez advised, then quickly added to her statement. "You shouldn't be able to run into anything. In theory, while in the FTL state you should not interact with mass traveling at non-FTL velocities."

"I don't know about you, Colonel, but I'd sure hate to be the one who found out that theory was wrong."

Gutierrez smiled. "Sorry, Commander. If it's any consolation, you seem capable of handling anything you run into. As long as it's not a real big rock."

"Thanks," Josh snorted, then glared directly at Colonel Gutierrez. "Look, Colonel, I'm about to risk my life, and despite everybody telling me about how capable I am I've yet to get a straight answer on why I was picked for this job."

"You're a very level-headed, very capable individual," she recited, avoiding his gaze.

"Thanks, again. I must be the most capable guy on Earth. But that's not the reason. Why, Colonel? Why me instead of somebody like you? You're a pilot, with the training and reflexes to handle something moving fast. Me, I'm a ship-driver by training. I got picked for NASA because they needed people who could keep space station systems running, and ship-board training seemed to be a useful equivalent. So, why me?"

Colonel Gutierrez didn't answer for a moment, staring into the emptiness outside the hanger. "Because of what you said,

Commander. You're not a pilot. Listen. The first six probes never came back. They've spent years analyzing the theory, the mechanical systems, the technology, the training. Nothing seems wrong. Nothing explains the failures. But we assume that on the other side of FTL things are going to be strange. We've just talked about that. So the human factor will be critical. After analyzing every aspect of the first six missions, we could find only one major factor the first six pilots had in common."

Horton took a deep breath. "And that was?"

"They were all pilots." Gutierrez shook her head angrily. "Maybe that's it. Maybe something in our training is leading us astray. Maybe. It's our best guess, our only guess, right now."

"Great." Josh stared at the bright displays on the probe's control panel, reaching out to slowly tap one of the two mechanical clocks ticking silently away, then glanced at the triple-redundant mechanical watch attached to his wrist. "Our best guess. Okay. At least that tells me something. They've built in mechanical back-ups to every electrical component they could, just in case FTL messes it all up. But humans only come in one standard configuration, don't they?"

"They come in many configurations, Commander. As many configurations as there are ways of seeing things. Pilots are one configuration. You may be a different enough configuration to make a difference."

"Colonel, I sure as hell hope you're right about that."

* * *

The shuttle, which Josh couldn't keep from thinking of as a tug, released the clamps holding the Prometheus probe in place. Pushed well away from the space station, facing into eternal emptiness, the probe ran its final automated checks before initiating the test flight.

Josh Horton watched lights flick on and off and digits cycle rapidly as the onboard computers checked and rechecked every component. He tried not to think about the flight, running through scenes from his favorites movies as the countdown dragged, but found his gaze repeatedly wandering back to the displays and to the mechanical linkage to the FTL drive which should drop the probe into normal state if the electrical timer failed to send the signal. Finally, every marker glowed green, every read-out matched required parameters. Horton cleared his throat, acutely aware that his next words might be the last anyone else would ever hear from him. "This is Prometheus Seven. All checks complete. Preparing to initiate test flight."

"Roger, Prometheus Seven. You are cleared for test flight initiation. Begin count-down on my mark." Horton raised one hand over the mechanical back-up timer, ready to mash it down at the same moment the electronic timer began counting down. "Mark." Horton's hand fell, and both mechanical timer and its electrical counterpart began scrolling off what could be the last ten seconds of his life.

Zero. Prometheus Seven flexed as if the entire probe were ballooning, its structure booming like a deep-throated bell. A moment later a secondary but still powerful crash marked the probe's guts collapsing back into place. Josh Horton felt his own body flex strangely in time to the probe's agony, jarring his senses unlike anything he'd every experienced. *Some kind of shock wave when this thing transitioned to FTL, even though it's probably not a wave. Got to check the equipment. That had to mess up something.*

Everything he tried to look at was oddly hazed, almost wavering in blurry imprecision. Josh shook his head violently, blinking in rapid succession, but the instrument panel before him remained blurred. *Did that shock mess up my sight or is this how things look when you're moving faster than light? How am I going to tell if that shock knocked anything off-line? It must have messed up the backup mechanical linkages.* He squinted, trying to focus. The read-outs remained fuzzy, but several resolved themselves into the same digits they'd held when he started. A close examination of the mechanical linkage showed it blurred in places but also apparently in the same configuration. The viewscreens showed as black blurs sprinkled with dancing spots of light.

Josh raised his arm to look at the watch on his wrist, staring in shock as the limb seemed to move in slow stop-motion jerks. A sudden sense of pressure on his wrist was followed by the realization that his watch was now pressed up against his helmet's face shield. *Faster-than-light speed. That must be it. My nervous system commands and feedback are moving slower than my environment. Just got to do things in stages. Allow time for feedback.*

Wrist and watch were still blurred, but by concentrating Josh made out the hour and minute hands on the watch face even though the second hand remained too vague to see. As best he could tell, no time had elapsed. *Okay. That makes sense. It's surely been less than a minute since I punched into FTL.* He fought back a sudden wave of nausea, closing his eyes against the churning in his gut and a growing headache. *Dizzy. I'm dizzy. Must be because of the incredible speed I'm traveling. Or maybe that shock messed up my brain, like getting kicked in the head. That'd explain the way everything I see is blurred.*

He focused back on the watch, which still displayed no apparent change. *It has to have been a minute by now. It has to.* The image remained stubbornly unchanged, the minute hand wavering in his sight like everything else, but apparently unmoved. *How much has this disorientation messed up my sense of elapsed time? Maybe I can count down in my head –* Another surge of nausea hit, stronger, the world seeming to spin in time to the thunder of his pulse in his head. *Got to beat this. Whether it's FTL effect or not, I can't function when I'm this dizzy. Okay. Got to spot something.* He knew that, knew from watching Miller and Kelly spin around dozen of times without falling, that dancers in movies had kept their balance through those spins by focusing on a single point as long as possible, then whipping their heads around to focus back on the same point. A fixed visual reference. Like looking at the horizon to fight sea-sickness.

Josh locked his eyes on one segment of the instrument panel, a blurry section where four displays met in what should have been a point. But the point remained too vague to make out, and the nausea kept growing. Flashes of false light flickered inside Horton's eyes as the dizziness gnawed at his consciousness. *Can't keep this up.* The displays all showed the same data, his wrist watch the same time. *Hasn't it been a minute yet? It has to have been!* The image of the watch seemed to fuzz a little more, but remained stubbornly unchanged. He concentrated on the instrument readouts again, seeing vague numbers which all seemed to add up to normal states.

The instruments say everything's fine. Everything's not fine. Why am I so dizzy? Just seeing things blurry shouldn't make me dizzy. I know people who need glasses who don't get disoriented just because they're not wearing them. Sure I'm moving incredibly fast, but how can my brain know that when it doesn't have anything to look at that says I'm moving fast? Wait a minute. Josh fought down another wave of disorientation, trying to dredge up the memory which had teased him. *That story I told the Colonel about. The brain doesn't like what it sees. Makes up a picture. Blurry? Could this be a case of that happening? But I'm seeing the instruments. They say everything's fine…there was something else. Something really important.*

His heart pounding in time to his head, Josh barely kept from throwing up as he fought to recover the memory he sought. *I gotta remember. Something that might be the key to this…keys. That was… yeah. The brain makes up a picture when it can't handle what the optic system sends it. But that picture only shows what the brain expects to see. You don't see your car keys on the desk you whip your eyes across because the brain doesn't know the keys are there and so doesn't put them in the picture it makes up. But what would that –. Oh, my God.*

Horton blinked again, vainly trying to focus on his blurred instruments. *Am I really seeing these? I'm moving faster than light. My eyes and brain evolved to work with light-speed messages. My eyes are seeing something now, but what? Is it images my visual system can't handle, like that blank spot? If it is, then my brain's just making all this up. It's showing me what it expects to see, because it can't accept what it does see. It's showing me instruments which say everything is fine because that's what it remembers. It's showing me an intact mechanical linkage because that's what it remembers.*

He moved his arm again, sweating from fear and discomfort, trying to maintain concentration while his brain spun wildly. Stop-motion jerks brought his hand to the FTL control, then he slammed it down even as his consciousness ebbed.

Josh gradually became aware of his breathing, shuddering, eyes tightly closed as the world still spun inside. He forced his eyes open, blurred metal above them, causing his heart to pound again, but this time the metal resolved into firm detail when he concentrated. Lowering his gaze, he stared at the instrument panel. One screen displayed the outside, endless stars marching away. In a corner, the navigational system was running an analysis, trying to match the stars it could see with the picture expected an appreciable fraction of a light year from home.

His wristwatch showed almost ten minutes gone by. According to the electronic readouts, slightly less than four minutes had elapsed. *So, best guess, I was in FTL state for six minutes. And the electronic timers didn't work in that state. Ugly. What about the mechanical back-up?* Horton bent to view the linkage, shuddering as he spotted a component drifting loose. *Broke off during that transition shock, I'd guess. The mechanism didn't have enough flexibility at that point.* The navigation system chirped happily, displaying the probe's estimated position. Horton stared, dread fighting with elation as he saw the system read-out declaring him to be approximately twenty-four light minutes from his start-point. *Wow. This baby's even hotter than they thought. I must have been going six times the speed of light. In terms of distance from home I just beat Magellan and Columbus all to hell. Now, how do I get* back *home?*

* * *

"You used chewing gum?" Colonel Gutierrez demanded, her voice over the communications circuit sounding disbelieving.

"I had some with me," Josh explained. The probe drifted, awaiting rendezvous with the shuttle sent to retrieve it. "My mouth gets dry sometimes when I'm tense, you know, so I usually carry gum. It worked to repair the broken link, and was flexible enough to handle the shock when I went back into FTL to get home."

"And that was why we lost the other six probes? Because of a single broken linkage?"

"No, Colonel." Josh tried to keep his voice unemotional, tried not to think of the six pilots before him who had ridden into oblivion. "We lost those probes because they were being controlled by pilots. Your guess was right."

"I don't understand," Colonel Gutierrez shot back in anger. "Why do you say that? What would pilots have done differently?"

"Colonel, they'd have done something fundamentally different. Because they were pilots. Because of their training," Horton explained carefully. "I'm not a pilot, but I know plenty of them. You're trained to trust your instruments, right?"

"Of course."

"Especially when you're disoriented, right? And lacking outside visual reference?"

"Naturally! It's when you're disoriented that you most need to refer to your instruments. You have to follow what they tell you or you'll crash. It's too easy to mistake what you think you see…" The Colonel's words trailed off. "I think I understand."

"Yeah. Pilots' training tells them that they must depend on what their instruments tell them when they get disoriented. It's drilled into them, isn't it? The better the pilot, the more experienced and the more highly trained, the more they know to depend on their instruments. Right?"

"Right." Colonel Gutierrez sounded as if she were in agony.

"But at FTL you're not seeing those instruments you're trying to depend on," Josh continued. "You're seeing an image generated by your brain. Blurred. Incomplete. And consisting only of whatever the brain remembers seeing from before or is otherwise convinced must be true. I thought I saw an intact linkage when there was actually a broken one there. I thought the instruments were saying everything was working fine. But you can't trust anything you see in FTL state. Or rather, anything you think you see."

"Like Alice," Colonel Gutierrez murmured. "Down the Rabbit Hole into a world where nothing is what it looks to be. Wait a moment. Didn't you report you saw your arm move, even though the vision came in jerks?"

"I thought I did. Most likely, what I really saw was my brain knowing I'd moved my arm, getting feedback from the muscles, and calculating where I ought to see it based on how much it had moved. That's what made the picture stop-motion. I guess our brain's image-manufacturing center can't handle streaming video very well."

"That makes sense. But why were you different, Commander? What made you act against what your instruments were telling you?"

Josh shrugged, unseen by his listener. "Me? I got my training on ships. I don't trust instruments any further than I have to trust them. I assume stuff isn't going to work right. That training saved my butt. But pilots have to train and act differently."

"Pilots have to train and act in ways that keep them alive on Earth," Colonel Gutierrez stated bleakly, "but in ways that will apparently kill them in FTL state. What happened to them, Commander Horton? What do you think happened to the pilots we sent before you?"

"The transition shock surely knocked their mechanical linkages off-line just like happened to my probe. After that, I think they kept referring to their instruments as long as they could, probably seeing things on the displays that their brains said ought to be there if they were getting so dizzy, until they passed out. Any corrective actions wouldn't have worked because they were based on imaginary instrument displays. If the pilots started to recover, they'd just get disoriented again and pass out again. So their probes just kept going."

"Like being caught in a high-speed spin forever," Gutierrez noted bitterly. "Damn. Damn it all. Why did they have to die like that?"

Horton sighed heavily, shaking his head. "Because you can theorize about something and observe something from a distance and plan for something, but you never really know what's it like until you go there for real. That's why we need explorers, Colonel."

"And explorers don't always come back, do they?"

"No. They don't."

"We should have sent robotic probes! I told them! We could have designed enough fail-safe's in to each one so that eventually a probe would have reported back with the answer. We didn't have to risk humans on blind thrusts into the unknown!"

Horton paused for a moment, thinking. "I'm sorry, Colonel, but you're wrong. You know what saved me? Ginger Rogers."

"Ginger Rogers? The actress?"

"The dancer, Colonel. You know, I didn't get it right earlier when I said my professional training made the difference. That was only part of it. The other part was the old movies and the science programs I like to watch."

"I don't understand."

"They're what told me what was wrong. Movies and random bits of learning. What made the difference were things I picked up in the course of living, little bits of apparently unrelated information that came from being a human being with a life of varied experiences behind me. You see, Colonel? Those robotic systems you just talked about. How would we have known to incorporate the knowledge they'd need to realize what was wrong and why? Who the heck would have programmed a robotic explorer with what would have been regarded as useless trivia? But that kind of knowledge, the stuff a person just happens to pick up because people like to do that, that's what made the difference." Josh paused, remembering the overwhelming mix of exhilaration and loneliness he'd felt at being further from home than any human in history, imagining a machine in the same place, seeing the same things but feeling nothing. "Besides, we've got a universe to explore. Why would we want to let robots have all the fun?"

AUTHOR'S NOTE
GENERATION GAP

Once it became clear just how far distant other stars were, and how long it would take for a human spacecraft to cross that distance, the idea of generation ships was born. The trip might take many human lifetimes, but that could be handled by having a ship in which the crew was made up of families. As the original members aged, they would train the next generation, who would run the ship while giving birth to and training the generation after them, and so on until the immensely-long voyage was done. The typical science fiction story about generation ships has something going wrong. Part of the crew mutinies, critical equipment breaks, the crew forgets they are even on a ship, and so on. But it is possible that a system can be devised which is so strong, so effective in maintaining order and the equipment on the ship that the ship would reach its objective safely. At that point, a system that strong might itself become the problem.

GENERATION GAP

"Is it real?" From the observation deck of the Generation Ship Terra, a compartment of cold, gray metal relieved only by wide display screens, the blue/white/brown world below seemed like one more video simulation played out within the confines of the ship's computer systems.

"It's real." Greg Tyre nodded toward the image. "I went to one of the airlocks, suited up, and went Outside for a look. It's there."

Frowns creased brows all around him as the crowd reacted. "Was your walk authorized?"

"Why does that -?" Greg bit off his reply as he saw the frowns deepening. "Yes. I'm a ship maintenance and repair tech. I can authorize a walk whenever needed to examine the hull. I determined it was needed."

Most of the frowns disappeared at the reassurance and attention returned to the globe on the displays. Greg turned at a touch on his sleeve and saw Jane Fernandez had come up next to him. She leaned close to whisper. "Oh, dear. You might have broken a Rule, Mr. Tyre."

"Yeah," he murmured back. "Why get manic over that when we're looking at the planet our great-grandparents set out to reach?"

His answer came not from Jane but from a large man who shook his head, eyes narrow with disapproval. "Those Rules kept us alive and got us here, young man. Continue conforming to them."

Greg smiled back at the man. "Yissur." The man glowered at the youthful slurring of the respectful reply, made a clear show of reading Greg's nametag, then turned his back.

Greg felt a tug on his sleeve, following as Jane led the way out of the crowded compartment. As they closed the hatch behind them, Jane pointed back inside, made a gagging motion, then laughed. "I am going to be soooo glad to get off this thing. What do you suppose it'll be like?"

"A planet? Like the simulations, I guess."

"Oh, get real. It's got to be different. Come on, let's go to Port One and watch the screen there."

Port One, the first recreation lounge on the left side of the ship, displayed the same image on its display screen. A crowd of young men and women were scattered at the tables, eyeing the vision with rapt attention. "Hey, Jane. Greg," one hailed them. "It looks like Earth, doesn't it?"

Jane shook her head. "Different land masses."

"I don't mean in *details*."

"Then don't ask a planetary geologist for an opinion." Jane laughed again as she took a seat. "I still can't believe it. A real planet where I can actually practice geology."

Greg smiled and nodded. "Yeah. It's weird. We've been scheduled to arrive here about this time ever since our great-grandparents set off. But it never seemed real, not until we actually got here."

"It still doesn't -" Jane's reply was cut off by the image of the planet vanishing, replaced by the Seal of the Community of Terra Township and a loud fanfare of trumpets. "Oh, hell. What's Mayor Magetry got to say?"

The community seal slowly faded in time to the trumpets, replaced by the lined face of Mayor Magetry. Magetry looked slowly back and forth, as if scanning his audience, which he could indeed be doing if he chose to use the surveillance cameras in every compartment. "This is a good day." A low groan emitted from the young adult audience in Port One. Magetry had begun every speech of his career as mayor with that phrase, and since he'd been continuously reelected since his father stepped down, it had been a long career. "We have fulfilled the dreams of our ancestors by reaching this planet."

Jane cocked an eyebrow at Greg. "I thought our ancestors' dream was to establish a colony here."

"Me, too."

Magetry's face held a warning frown, now. "I must caution against irrational exuberance, against any weakening of the bonds and Rules and Traditions which have kept us happy and healthy over this long journey. The planet must be examined. Evaluated. A landing party will be sent out after due time. Until then, continue in your duties, praise our ancestors, and trust in the procedures which have brought us this far, and will take us further. If need be." Magetry's face spasmed in a brief smile, then faded out to another trumpeted chorus.

"Inspiring," Greg noted. "Why is that robotic assist the mayor, anyway?"

"Because he's always been mayor," Jane pointed out. "Just like his daddy."

"Yeah. Mayor-for-Life Magetry. Heaven forbid the voters should elect anyone else. They've always voted for a Magetry. Why change?"

Jane grinned and called out the question to the crowd. "Why change?"

The other young adults in the room smiled with the same mixture of mockery and bitterness as the crowd yelled back: "It's always been that way!"

Someone pounded on the controls to the display until the image of the new world reappeared. While a few, brief cheers rang out, Carl Chang came in, spotted Greg and Jane, and headed for their table. "Private party?"

"Nope. Have a seat. How's life in social paralysis?"

Carl managed to look pained. "Social programs, if you please."

"Same difference."

"Not to me." Carl looked around conspiratorially. "I caused a real ruckus in there, you know. I moved somebody's pencil box to the other side of their desk."

"Don't let Magerty find out," Jane advised. "Did you hear his little speech about irrational exuberance?"

"I couldn't miss it. What'd you expect Magerty to say?"

"I dunno. Some hint he's happy about reaching the planet we've been heading for all our lives, maybe?"

Carl shrugged. "Why should he be happy?"

Greg gave him a puzzled look. "I'd think that was obvious."

"That's 'cause you're young. At least in ship terms. You're, what, close to thirty years old? Change isn't totally scary to you. I'll bet it'll be a lot scarier when you actually encounter change."

"What's so bad about change? I'm sick of Rules, sick of Traditions, sick of having people watching me every second to make sure I'm not deviating from the social norm."

Jane nodded. "Ditto."

Carl spread his hands in a gesture of helplessness. "Look, you guys are always joking about my job in social programs. But all I'm doing is helping to carry out the original vision for this ship. As are the people who are watching you. You know what the Terra is, right? I mean, as a social unit?"

"Paralyzed." Greg pointed at the display. "Did you view the last update we got from Earth? I couldn't even understand some of the stuff they were doing and talking about, until I saw some five minute segment of people who acted and talked like us. And you know what? That segment was part of a popular *historical* drama that's all the rage back on Earth these days."

Carl nodded, obviously unsurprised. "Sure. Like you say, we're paralyzed. By design. What do you get when put a few thousand humans into a social unit and isolate them? You get a small town. The most socially conservative way of living known to mankind.

Small towns don't change, because the social pressure is all aimed at conformity. That us. Change comes to small towns as a result of outside influences. New people moving in, new ideas coming in. How much of that do we have?"

"None."

"Right. We live like our great-grands did, because there's nothing forcing us to change." Carl leaned forward, speaking softly. "Even ideas. The updates from Earth get censored, you know."

"Everybody's heard that."

"Because it's true. Don't let any disturbing stuff enter the community. And guess what? Most of our little community is as happy as can be with that." Carl chuckled. "There's also the social system whereby people marry and have kids late. That's why people our age are regarded as 'young.' It all builds stability. People used to worry about breakdown in social order on generation ships like this one. But, really, they tend to the exact opposite. Social stability."

"And," Jane added, "if they start to veer from that, social programs gets them back on track."

"Um, yeah."

"Do you ever feel guilty?"

"A little. People can be happy without being happy in a socially conforming way. But not on a ship where carelessness or accident or riot could literally kill us all. Which is why we have Rules instead of just rules." Carl smiled briefly at the displayed image of the new world. "But, down there, we can relax, I guess. Maybe I won't feel any duty to keep people in line."

"What'll you do, instead?"

"Try to help people like Magerty cope, maybe."

"I'm sure he's planning on running that planet just like he's run the Terra all our lives." Greg smiled at the thought. "But down there we'll be able to leave if we want. Form our own town if we want."

Carl seemed disconcerted by the thought. "I...suppose. But it'll be just a few thousand humans against a whole world, you know. We'll need to stick together. Do what's best for everyone."

Jane eyed Carl appraisingly. "You sound like an elder. A conforming elder. As Greg and I were just saying, our ancestors' objective was to establish a human colony in another star system. It wasn't to keep things from ever changing in our society."

"I explained -."

"Something we already knew. We had to do it to stay alive and keep the ship from breaking apart. Fine. We made it."

Carl smiled once again. "Hey, no offense. I understand. Will you be going down with the survey missions?"

"I hope so." Jane's attention swung back to the image of the world below. "I can't wait."

* * *

"Why are *you* going instead of me?"

Greg smiled in what he hoped was a placating manner. "All I know is the shuttle pilot wants a maintenance tech along, and I got picked. Really, Jane. I had nothing to do with it."

"It's not fair!" She glowered at him, then spun on her heel to stomp away. "At least bring me back a rock!" Jane yelled over her shoulder.

"Sure. No problem," Greg assured her back just before she left the room. He took a deep breath, checked his tool kit, then headed for the shuttle docking bay.

"Tyre? I'm Trey. Shuttle pilot." A woman perhaps two decades older than Greg stuck out a hand and grinned. "I've gotten some of your stuff because of typos."

"Is that why you picked me?"

"Partly. I was familiar with the fact you existed. But I also wanted someone young enough to still be able to think independently."

"Excuse me?"

The pilot raised her eyebrows. "You don't understand?"

"Well, yeah. I just didn't expect that from, uh…"

"And old broad? I'm not that old, kid. And I'm a pilot, which means I value having someone with a good brain backing me up." She shook her head, gazing at the airlock leading to the shuttle bay. "You can train somebody to the point they stop thinking. Yeah, you do understand, don't you? All we've ever dealt with on the Terra are the same things, over and over again. I expect to deal with something new on that planet."

Greg smiled. "I sure hope so, ma'am."

"Give me a break. I'm not that old. It's Gayle." She checked her watch. "Come on. The schedule of events calls for our passengers to arrive in exactly twenty minutes, so I'm sure that's exactly when they'll all show up. Let's get some checks done."

The airlock felt no different from any of the airlocks Greg had used to access the outside of the Terra's hull, but instead of open space it led into the bay of the shuttle. A dozen seats, six to a side, filled the upper part of the bay, while a hatch labeled 'cargo' led to a lower area. Gayle Trey led the way forward through another hatch into the small cockpit, then indicated the seat next to her. "That's the flight mechanic's position. Strap in tight when the time comes."

"Yes, ma'am. Sorry."

"You'll get over it. So will I." She rubbed her cheeks with both palms, eyeing the navigational display. "We've been surveying the planet from orbit since we arrived, you know. We'll be landing on a plain not far from a major river. It's in what should be the planet's temperate zone, and looks well suited for a colony." Gayle grinned indulgently at Greg, who suddenly realized he had a huge smile on his face. "Really looking forward to it, huh?"

"You bet."

A chime announced the arrival of the passengers. "Wait here."

Greg pretended to study the instruments while Gayle led the survey team into the shuttle bay, then frowned as he heard a sharp voice. "Rules require the senior qualified mechanic in cases such as this."

"No, they don't," Gayle replied in a polite but unyielding tone. "The Rules state the senior qualified individual should be used *if* all other factors are equal. As pilot for this mission, I decide whether all other factors are indeed equal. It is my judgment that Mechanic Tyre is best qualified, and the Rules give my judgment priority."

Mumbles, grumbles and the rattle of seat harnesses being fastened were the only other sounds until Gayle returned and sealed the hatch. "You ready? she asked Greg.

Greg belatedly realized he hadn't strapped himself in and fumbled with the straps, trying to sort out the tangle. "Blast it."

"It's not that complicat*ed.*" Greg flushed as he saw Gayle watching him with an amused expression. "A bit nervous?"

"Hell, yes."

"Me, too. I've never actually flown this thing in atmosphere or a planetary gravity field. Just simulations. It ought to be interesting to see how accurate the simulations are, huh?"

Greg's eyes widened. "Uh, yeah."

She checked some readings on the panel before her, then smiled thinly. "Every month I've come in here and run system checks. Every month. Just like my dad did. Just like his mother did. Now I finally get to use it. I get to *do* something with it."

"It sounds like you're looking forward to it."

"Damn straight. Let's go."

Greg's stomach protested the shuttle's movement. A lifetime on the massive Terra hadn't prepared him for the lurches and swings of a much smaller craft. He gulped, praying he wouldn't lose his last meal, and glanced over at the pilot. Gayle sat, her eyes locked on the display, her hands gripping the controls ever so lightly.

The shuttle skipped across the upper atmosphere, shedding velocity and losing altitude, the outside image on the display growing wavery as turbulence and heat distorted the view. Gayle pushed the shuttle lower, easing up slightly as its structure vibrated under the strain. The sky grew bluer, the land more defined. Something white shot by in a flash, startling Greg, then another. "Clouds," Gayle breathed, like someone who'd just seen a miraculous vision.

Greg fought down a wave of panic as the planet's surface jumped toward them. Gayle touched the controls gently, correcting the shuttle's approach to the open field, as grass and other vegetation shot by close underneath. The forward braking thrusters fired, reducing the landing velocity, then the shuttle transitioned to hover before gently coming to rest.

Greg waited impatiently while the survey team painstakingly tested the planet's atmosphere. The atmosphere had already been sampled a dozen times by automated probes, but none of the team seemed willing to trust that data. Finally, the leader signaled approval and the shuttle's exterior hatch was cracked.

"What do you think?" Gayle had followed Greg out of the shuttle and stood beside him now, staring around.

"It's…overwhelming." New sights, new sounds, views running off to an horizon which seemed impossibly distant. "I've been in Earth-based sims, but this is…is…so much more."

"Yeah." She bent to feel the grass-like stalks beneath their feet, then jumped backwards as something small and grayish scuttled away from her hand. "A bug! Look! A bug!"

"Really?" It looked like the pictures he'd seen of bugs, anyway, though Greg had an impression of ten legs instead of six before the creature vanished into the surrounding field. "Does it bite?"

"It didn't bite me."

A shout echoed from where the survey team had huddled together. "Look out!" The team scattered in all directions, one member waving frantically toward Gayle and Greg. "Life forms! Insectile life forms! Look out! They're in the grass!"

"I guess they found a bug, too," Greg remarked. He eyed the ground uneasily, shifting his feet. "How many are there? Am I standing on one?"

Gayle took a step back onto the shuttle's ladder. "Maybe. Hey!"

She swung one hand in a frantic motion as a small, gray object fluttered erratically near her head. "Another bug. A flying one. Bug repellent. We need bug repellent."

"That's right. We have the formula for that, don't we? If it works on bugs here." Greg brushed his hair back in annoyance as a breeze flipped it over his eyes. "Somebody's got the vent fans set too high."

"Vent fans?"

"Yeah, the -. Oh. That's, uh, wind, right?"

"Right. It sets its own speed." Gayle squinted around. "Annoying, isn't it? I want to turn it down, too. Setting up house on a plain might not be a good idea if wind's a problem. What's that shining over there?"

Greg followed her gaze. "Water, I think. Isn't that where that river is?"

"Uh huh. Good call."

Several survey team members came to cluster near the shuttle, one nervously staring toward the river as well. "That's dangerous, you know."

"Dangerous?" Greg questioned.

"Running water. Rapids. Undertows. Aquatic predators. Mud flats. Very dangerous."

"It looks sort of pretty from here."

"So does a neutron star from a distance. That doesn't mean you want to get near it."

"Floods," another stated.

"Right. Rivers can flood. Maybe we want to be someplace higher. The mountains? Aren't there fewer insects in the mountains?"

The first surveyor checked his data unit. "Yes. At least, that was the case on Earth. But it's colder in the mountains. And, uh, landslides."

"Landslides?"

"Falling rocks and soil. And snowslides. Same thing, in winter."

The surveyors headed slowly away from the shuttle again, scanning the grass as they carefully placed each foot.

Greg watched them, then jerked back as another bug zipped past his face. "Gayle? Do we have any of that bug repellent on the shuttle?"

"I sure hope so. Let's find out."

"I wonder why we didn't think to put it on before we left the shuttle?"

"Probably for the same reason we didn't think to wear hats." Gayle squinted into the sun. "That's a little too bright to be comfortable, too. Maybe we could get, uh…"

Another surveyor, gingerly walking past, looked over at her. "Sunburn. Yes. Painful."

"How do you know if you're getting sunburn?"

"Check your first aid manual for depictions of radiation burns. A sunburn is simply a relatively mild form of radiation burn. And that means it can lead to skin cancer. You should minimize exposure."

"Radiation burns? Just from walking around?" Greg shaded his eyes. "Is there anything down here that isn't dangerous or annoying?"

The surveyor paused, as if taking the question absolutely seriously. "We're still checking the planet out."

Some hours later, the surveying team gathered back at the shuttle. Some of them, those with the fairest skins, showed the blush of what the alarmed medical team member announced to be the first traces of sunburn. An additional hour was spent exhaustively searching for bugs which might be hiding in anyone's clothing or equipment. The flight back proved uneventful, more tiring than exciting after the labors of the past hours. Yet, as the survey team filed off the shuttle and back into the hull of the Terra, their spirits obviously rose. "We're back!" the team leader announced happily. "Everyone, get your reports filed as soon as possible."

Greg watch them leave. "Gayle?"

"Yeah, kid?"

"Back on the planet, those team members looked unhappy and uncomfortable the entire time. Now, they couldn't be happier."

"What'd you expect? They're home."

Greg looked around at the metal making up the surfaces all around. "Yeah, but…not anymore. We have to think of that planet as home."

"That's not going to be easy, Greg. Even for younger types."

* * *

"How long are they going to take to evaluate this planet?" Jane demanded. "It's been three weeks since you went down and nothing's happened. They haven't even staged one of their stupid contests, like 'let's name the planet.'"

Greg shook his head. "I don't know that any more than you do."

"At least I have my rock. Thanks for bringing that back, anyway." She slapped the table top. "They haven't even sent down any more survey teams! They're just analyzing and reanalyzing the stuff gathered by the first team."

"The automated probes on the surface are still sending back data -."

"If we wanted to examine this world by automated probes then humans didn't need to come out here in the first place!" Jane subsided, then glanced around Port One. "Where's your buddy Carl?"

"I thought he was your buddy, too."

"Well…where's he been?"

"I heard from him real briefly. Apparently you're not the only one chafing at the bit to get on the planet. Social programs is working overtime to keep everyone calm, productive and happy."

"Ugh. I'm sorry, Greg, I used to like Carl a lot, too, but the more I think about his job…"

"I know. But Carl's doing it for good reasons. He doesn't buy into it as an end-all like the elders in social programs."

"He didn't when he started out. That was years ago."

Greg frowned down at the table. "I don't think he's changed that much."

"You -. Who's that?"

Greg followed Jane's gaze to where a woman had entered the room, her maturity making her stand out next to the twenty-somethings who usually frequented the lounge. "Gayle Tyre. The shuttle pilot who took us down to the planet. She's good people, Jane."

"I remember you told me that. What's she doing here? Did she take a liking to you or something?"

"She's a little bit older than me, Jane."

"Some women like that. So do some men."

"Not this one. Besides, I prefer planetary geologists to pilots. I got you a rock, didn't I?"

"Be still my heart."

The pilot scanned the tables until her eyes settled on Greg. Gayle beckoned Greg silently, eyed Jane for a moment appraisingly, then gestured her along as well. Greg and Jane exchanged glances, then rose to follow the pilot out of the lounge. They walked swiftly and silently through a procession of hatches and passageways until they reached a small compartment whose walls were lined with shelves holding pieces of equipment. When Gayle had sealed the hatch behind them, she waved around. "Junkyard. Stuff that can't be fixed and has been stripped of everything worth cannibalizing."

Greg stared around in amazement. "It can't be fixed?"

"This ship's a closed system. Eventually, even our stockpiles run low, even our repair and fabrication facilities run out of certain materials. And, no, the general populace isn't told. It might cause 'alarm.'"

"Why'd you bring us here?"

"Because the surveillance gear in this room is also busted. It's been cannibalized to keep the cameras and mikes going in other rooms, where seditious youngsters like yourselves gather." The pilot slumped against the nearest wall. "The town council's made a decision."

"About what?"

"The future. Their's and our's. The planet's been declared unsuitable for habitation."

"What?" Jane seemed to be in shock. "Why?"

"All kinds of reasons. Weather. Mercy, it can rain down there. Or get cold. Or hot. The wind blows. Right, Greg? Bugs. Animals. Plants growing all over the place. Tectonic activity. You might get earthquakes."

"That's just like Earth!"

"It's not being judged by people who've ever lived on Earth, young lady. It's being judged by people who've spent their entire lives, like their parents before them, inside a world where the temperature is always maintained at a comfortable level, there's no bugs in the beds, the plants are all kept in pots and the only storms are emotional."

"But…but…" Jane looked at Greg helplessly. "Any planet will be like that. Any livable planet. They can't evaluate a living world by the criteria of a climate-controlled ship!"

Gayle grimaced. "You saw them, Greg. On the surface. How'd most of the landing party react?"

"As if they'd been dropped into the first-stage recycling tanks. I sort of understood that. I mean, it was all so uncontrolled. So wild. But they were looking for a reason to reject the world, anyway, weren't they?"

"Yeah. You're pretty smart for a kid." Gayle grinned at the mocking reference to Greg's relative youth. "Those reasons are just an excuse. They don't want to change. Anything."

Jane stared at the pilot. "Like Carl told us. Stability is the primary virtue, the primary imperative, in the society of the Terra. Actually setting up a colony on that world would change everything, wouldn't it?"

"Oh, yeah. People who didn't like Mayor-for-Life Magetry could actually go somewhere else and set up their own town. The Rules wouldn't have to be Rules anymore." Gayle raised her hands as if grasping at invisible controls. "I could fly. Across a world. See new things. Let my kids fly, too, instead of endlessly training so their descendents could someday fly."

Greg remembered the air rushing past the shuttle's hull, the wild ride to the surface. "I can understand that."

"But it's more than that. Moving down onto that world means leaving this controlled, man-made little world of ours. We'd have to deal with lots of stuff that we can't control. Like weather, just to give one example. That's a big change for us, too."

"Our ancestors did that. So can we. Why are you telling us this?"

"Because I don't want to put up with it and I don't know what to do! I've been living on this ship too long. My brain's almost hard-wired. You guys can still think for yourselves, right?"

"How long have we got to think of something?"

"Twenty hours. That's how long it's supposed to take to get the course calculated and the main drives ready to propel the ship toward the secondary objective. Magerty and the others know some people will be unhappy with leaving here. They plan on announcing the decision just before they light off the drives so there's no time for anyone to do anything."

"The secondary objective." An alternate world in an alternate solar system. "It'll take the ship more generations to get there. We'd never see a planet again, would we?'

"No."

"And when the ship finally reaches that secondary world, who-ever's in charge then, Magerty the Sixth or Seventh or Tenth or whatever, will decide that's unsuitable, too, won't they? And try to head for some tertiary world."

"I'd bet on that, yeah."

"Just try to keep things the same. Until the ship breaks too bad to fix and our descendents die in the middle of nowhere." Greg found himself laughing, then noticed the expressions on the faces of the others. "It's so damned ironic. Our ancestors set this up. They wanted an extremely stable social environment. Nobody rocking the boat, nobody trying to change things, and all so their descendents could someday reach another world and establish a colony. But they forgot that their stable social system might backfire at the critical point. Why should a system built on stability want to change things? Especially when the ship they built is so predictable and comfortable compared to the conditions we'll encounter on the planet? They worked so hard to make sure it'd succeed that they set this colonization attempt up to fail."

"We follow the Rules," Gayle pointed out. "Our ancestors could have set a Rule that we had to land on the planet. No options."

"But what if the planet really had been some hell-hole? Then Magerty and all his supporters might be shoving us into the landers regardless of what the surveys found." Greg looked toward Jane. "We've got to do something."

"Something? What kind of something?" Jane waved around to indicate the rest of the ship. "We can't take over. The security force won't back us, and a majority of the people on board will either support Magerty or refuse to oppose him. Even a lot of the younger adults. Most people don't want to rock the boat. We don't have to take a poll. You *know* that's true."

"Yeah. I do. I'd guess anywhere from one quarter to one third of the people on the Terra would feel like we do and be willing to do something to actually oppose leaving." Greg looked away, his gaze focusing on a forlorn piece of equipment, broken beyond repair, perhaps doomed to sit in this room as long as the Terra existed. Just like the human inhabitants of the ship. Something he'd said earlier tugged at his mind. The landers. "Then we have to leave."

"Leave? Just accept Magerty's decision and sit while the Terra heads for another star system?"

"No. I mean we have to leave. Leave the ship."

"What?" Jane took a moment to let the thought sink in. "How?"

"The landers. We all got taught about them in school. The flight and landing sequences are automated. Each one's got a bunch of supplies and equipment on board. And they'll each carry a hundred people down, right? We just take a few."

"A few? How many do you think will go with us?"

"I don't know. And we have less than twenty hours to somehow collect a group of people who feel like we do without letting anybody know we're breaking the Rules."

Gayle shook her head. "That's not your only challenge. You can't just waltz onto the colony landers. There's interlocks and alarms and system passwords. Those need to be bypassed or isolated. The landers can be warmed up in about an hour's time if they're like the shuttles, but you need to keep the ship's control room from knowing you're doing that."

"What about the people we're leaving?" Jane asked. "If we take the landers, what happens to them?"

Gayle shrugged. "They'll be fine. There's enough landers to take down almost the entire population, and each of them has an assortment of redundant colonizing gear on board. They're one-way transport, remember? Only the shuttles were designed for multiple ground-to-space flights."

"Are we also taking one of the shuttles?"

"Damn right we are. That's mine."

Jane checked her watch. "Twenty hours. There's no way you and I and the few other people we can trust can sound out literally hundreds of other people to see who wants to go."

"We don't have to ask everybody -."

"We have to ask a lot of them! I don't want to leave someone who really wants to go. And we'll need every person we can get. We'll need them for their skills, and their ability to do manual labor, and just for simple genetic diversity. Right?"

Greg bit his lip. "There's only one way to do this. We handle it like a propagating message. I sound out two people, who each sound out two people, and so on."

Gayle frowned. "That's very risky. If the wrong person hears, we can be stopped."

"What else can we do? Besides, one virtue of life on the Terra is we *know* our neighbors. Look, we'll use a password. Nobody gets the password until whoever sounds them out is sure they're with us. Up to that point, the discussion can just be written off as discontent and Magerty will think that'll be undercut when the Terra leaves, right? But anyone we're sure of will get the password and be told that when they get it they need to head for the landers."

"So what's the password?"

Greg hesitated, thinking of how they'd be violating the Rules which had governed their entire lives, and leaving the controlled comfort of the Terra for a future of uncertainty and toil on the planet beneath them. "'Forbidden fruit.' That'll be the password that we're leaving."

* * *

The elder standing watch at the hull systems panel glanced down at Greg. "You found that problem, yet?"

"Almost."

"I hadn't noticed anything wrong."

"It showed up during a remote diagnostic." Greg tried to keep his voice calm, almost bored. "Maybe it was just an intermittent thing, or a false reading, but the Rules say you have to follow-up. Even if it is the middle of the night and I should be asleep with most everybody else."

"That's right. It's good to see you kids taking the Rules seriously."

Greg offered the watch stander a hopefully sincere-looking smile, then continued the careful job of bypassing the alert systems which would otherwise provide warning the landers were being accessed and powered up. A final connection, a final check, and he nodded with real satisfaction. "That's got it."

The elder was already losing interest. "Everything's okay, now?"

"Just how it needs to be." Greg left the area, trying to suppress a wild grin, then checked the time. Three hours. He'd already bypassed the secondary watch panel, as well as the panel in the main control room where an unacknowledged alert would eventually present itself. He headed for the lander access area.

"Jane? How's it going?"

His friend twitched wildly at the question, then glared at him. "Greg Tyre, do me the favor of not sneaking up on me!"

"Sorry. I've finished the alert bypasses."

"Great." She raised her data unit and punched in a command. "I've sent out the password. People should start showing up real soon. Gayle's already got people here ready to start warming the landers. Nobody asked what you were doing?"

"A couple of people. I gave them a remote problem detection story and they didn't question it."

Gayle Trey and a couple of others came to join them. "Why should they? Nobody makes waves on the Terra. Nobody breaks the Rules. Not if they know what's good for them and don't want to be shunned by their neighbors."

A short woman standing beside the pilot and dressed in the deep blue of the security forces smiled tightly. "And they'd usually get caught, because their neighbors would tell. Don't worry. I'm an old friend of Gayle's, and I'm on your side. I've seen how the Terra's society works from the enforcement side. I don't like it. I want my kids to have freedom."

Jane nodded. "Did you rig the surveillance systems for this area?"

"Yes. They're showing an endless loop of the last hour's recorded activity instead of actually monitoring the area. And since that hour included absolutely no activity, everything will look fine to my soon-to-be former co-workers."

Greg exhaled heavily, staring at the security woman. "I never thought of that. I guess we're lucky you're coming along."

Another smile. "I suppose so. You'll need cops on the surface, too, I expect."

A large man pushed his way forward. "Hopefully not." He glared around. "In case anybody cares, I've severed the control lines running from all remote locations to this area. Even if they find out what we're doing, they won't be able to stop us at the last minute by powering down the landers or something." Another glare. "I'm tired of people telling me what to do." The man turned and made his toward a lander entry bay.

Greg glanced at Jane and spoke softly so his voice wouldn't carry. "Did you see the look in that guy's eyes when he said he was tired of people telling him what to do?"

"Yeah. I guess freedom from conformity may have its downside in terms of some people."

People began arriving in the lander area, in small groups for the most part, including families urged on by one or both parents. All moved furtively, constantly glancing around. Gayle greeted a few, exchanging thumbs-up gestures. "More pilots. Good people to have," she advised Greg.

"I bet. I noticed a family resemblance."

"I told you my kids would get to fly."

"Have you noticed the ages of these people?"

"You mean the mix of elders and youth? Sure. There's more younger ones, but not everybody gets beaten into conformity by age." She eyed the stream of arrivals, biting her lower lip. "There's a lot. Has anybody been keeping count?"

Jane rubbed her forehead and consulted her data unit. "I've counted five landers filled and ready to go."

"Huh. And there's at least a couple of hundred more lining up. Looks like we might get up to a quarter of Terra's people. Cool."

Greg shook his head, staring at the people jostling into the access area. "Won't security see these people? I mean, they've got to be noticing all the traffic through the corridors."

"Depends if they're awake and watching or not. My friend the cop says they usually watch movies on this shift because nothing ever happens. And why should they expect anything different to happen tonight?"

"What if somebody told the wrong person?"

"If that'd happened, security'd already be here, right?"

"Or they'd be massing just out of sight."

The pilot shrugged. "If they charge, we slam the hatches and bolt. Too bad for those still outside, but I've no intention of letting the social programs people work me over."

"I can't blame you." Greg grimaced. "Social programs. There's somebody I forgot to tell."

Gayle checked her watch. "You've got maybe forty-five minutes before we're scheduled to go. But we might have to go earlier."

"I know. But I can't leave a friend."

Greg ran, along corridors which grew steadily more familiar, until he reached Carl's room. He hung on the buzzer until Carl, blinking sleep from his eyes, opened to door. "Carl. The town council decided to leave this planet and head for the secondary objective. We're bolting the Terra. Taking some landers. Come on."

Carl stared back at him. "You're not serious. Are you?"

"Yes! Come on. We're leaving soon."

"Wait a minute. Who's 'we'? How many people are you talking about?"

"I don't know exactly. Hundreds. Come on. This is our only chance for freedom, for change."

"Greg, if the council made the decision to leave, then they represent the entire populace. We have to respect that. We have to work together. No individual can put their wishes ahead of the group's, ahead of everyone else on the Terra."

Greg reached for Carl's arm. "Drop the social program cant, for heaven's sake. Let's go."

Carl's own hand came up and grabbed onto Greg's. "No. Let's go inside. Security has to know. It's for the best of everyone. Really."

"Let go of me!" Greg yanked back against Carl's grip, realizing as he did so that getting free would require a big fight, one certain to attract the attention of the security cameras monitoring this area. "Carl -."

"Greg, you can't do this."

A lifetime of resentment suddenly surged to the surface. "Don't tell me I can't make my own decisions, you son of a bitch!"

"I'm not -." Carl's eyes widened in surprise. Greg felt a smooth tube run next to his body, then Carl's body spasmed. Greg broke free, his own arm and hand tingling from the shock transmitted through Carl's grip, and turned to see Jane standing behind him with a security stun baton in one hand.

She stepped forward and jabbed the tip into Carl again, ensuring he was unconscious, then pushed his body inside and slid the door closed. "I told you so. Good thing Gayle told me you'd gone to get a friend, and I decided to come here in case this happened."

"Where'd you get that thing?"

"Gayle's security friend lent it to me. Come on. We've only got a few minutes left, even assuming this incident didn't attract anyone's attention."

They ran. An occasional person saw them, watching with curiosity as Greg and Jane hurtled by. As the entrance to the lander area came into view, they saw there were still a couple of dozen people funneling in. A moment later, pulsing red lights flared to life and speakers shouted out words which echoed through the quiet corridors. "Security alert. Security alert. Seal all hatches. All inhabitants of Terra remain in your current location. Warning. All landers are nonfunctional. I repeat, all landers are nonfunctional. Do not attempt to use them. Warning."

Gayle leaned out, her expression worried, then smiling as she spotted Greg and Jane. "What a relief. Get in here. Everybody!" she shouted, as some of the others hesitated in almost-instinctual obedience to the orders the speakers had given. One man paused, then turned and ran back the way he'd come. The others crowded in, Greg last. Gayle physically pulled him inside, pushing the hatch shut even as she did so. "They're right behind you. Get this thing sealed."

Greg put his shoulder to the hatch, helping her slam it shut, then hastily punched the button sealing the hatch tight. "How do we keep them from opening it before we get to the shuttle? They've got to have an override."

"They do," Gayle confirmed. "Jane, you still got that stun baton? Thanks." She popped the access on the hatch controls, shoved the baton's tip inside among the circuitry, then flinched as sparks and smoke flew. "Hopefully that'll buy us a few minutes. Let's go."

Another dash, across the short distance remaining to the shuttle bay, while the last families who'd made it inside hurled themselves into the nearest landers. The large man who'd boasted of severing the control links was standing in one lander's hatch, laughing in booming tones. "They tried to shut everything down! They couldn't! I stopped them! I finally beat the bastards!"

"Great," Gayle yelled. "Get in that lander and go!" She paused at the entrance to the shuttle, punching an intercom. "All landers depart immediately. Hit the launch control. The landers will seal their hatches and stagger their launches automatically. The landing area's already programmed in." She glanced back. "There goes that hatch."

Greg followed her look, watching as white hot metal flared away on all sides of the hatch. Off to one side, he could see some of the lander hatches sliding shut with agonizing deliberation. Then the closing airlock shut off his view and he was scrambling for a seat along with Jane and a few other stragglers.

The last buckle had barely been snapped when Gayle's voice sounded through the shuttle's intercom. "They're at the airlock. Everybody better be ready, because we're out of here!" The shuttle lurched, falling free from the Terra. "Okay, I see four, no, five landers already out. There goes number six. I don't think they can stop any of them, now."

In her seat, Jane seemed to be simultaneously laughing and sobbing. "We made it. We're free. We're free."

Greg stared at the shuttle's walls around him. Free? Somehow, that felt more different than anything he'd encountered on the planet they'd soon land on.

* * *

A long plume of light strung across the night sky, as if a comet were passing close to the planet. Greg stood silently watching that light, along with hundreds of others. The evening breeze felt milder than during his first visit to the planet, but also colder.

"They're leaving," Jane murmured. "They didn't even try to get us back. No promises. No threats. They're just leaving."

"They're probably glad to be rid of us. All the malcontents. Magerty's probably as happy as he's ever been."

"He can't be happy about losing the landers and all the supplies and equipment in them."

"It's not like he could've gotten them back. And all those supplies and equipment are to support a colony. Our colony."

"I guess." Jane lowered her gaze to the land around them. The wind made rushing noises as it passed around the bulk of the landers. Someone swore and slapped at an insect. "I hope those supplies include warmer clothes. It's a little cold."

"Yeah. Jackets and coats." He pulled her close. "I hope this helps for now."

"A little. What do we do now?"

"Figure out who's in charge. We'll need some sort of leadership.

Decide how to govern ourselves. Decide if this is the best place for the colony or if we should shift the landers. Gayle says they can lift long enough to move maybe a hundred kilometers if need be, and we probably want to be closer to a forest so we don't have to haul lumber a long ways. Get the lander incubators going for the animal zygotes in deep freeze -."

"Thanks, but I meant you and me when I said 'we.' Do you want to get married?"

"Sure, as soon as -." Greg smiled. "I was going to say, as soon as we both hit thirty. But we don't have to wait anymore, do we? That Rule's gone."

"Like a lot of others, I'm sure. Did we do the right thing, Greg? There's maybe a thousand of us here. Maybe a few more, but that's a lot smaller colony than the ancestors planned on, and we're completely on our own. What'll tomorrow bring, and the day after?"

"I don't know." He stared at her, then started laughing. "For the first time since I was born on the Terra, I don't know what tomorrow will bring. I don't know what I'll see. Isn't it great?"

She laughed, too, and hugged him. "Yeah. But I know one thing tomorrow will bring for sure."

"What's that?"

"I'm going to find some more rocks. I've got a lot to learn about this world our kids are going to inherit."

AUTHOR'S NOTE
KYRIE ELEISON

This ancient phrase actually predates Christianity and was incorporated into Christian worship, which is why "Kyrie Eleison" is the only Greek in the Latin Mass. It literally means "Lord Have Mercy" and was used to end prayers before being replaced by Amen. That impressed me, because I saw a humility in Kyrie Eleison, a recognition that we couldn't control the divine or compel it. Just, whatever You do, please have mercy on us. There always seem to be some people who claim to be especially favored, though, and sometimes when dealing with other people mercy seems too far from their thoughts.

KYRIE ELEISON

Frost rimmed the large, thick windows looking out over a cliff and down to dark water flecked by whitecaps. Sleet rattled against heavy stone walls as an erratic wind swept by. Low on the horizon, a reddish sun glowed through a rare small rent in the clouds that otherwise covered the sky, casting long shadows across the room where Garvis Skein lay abed, snoring heavily under the pile of blankets he favored for warmth.

Francesa walked quietly into the room, her uncovered feet making almost no sound, ignoring with the stoicism of years of experience the searing cold on the soles of her feet whenever she had to leave the comparative comfort of a rug's surface and cross bare stone. Working silently and swiftly, she pulled tinder and coal from the bag she carried and, kneeling in front of the stone fireplace in one corner, got a fire going with efficiency born of long practice.

Garvis stirred under his covers. Francesa froze, her breathing as shallow and quiet as possible. The fire popped, and Garvis' eyes opened, frowning at the ornate designs carved into the ceiling. The eyes slowly pivoted, coming to rest on Francesa. The man's eyes narrowed in annoyance. "You have broken a rule," he muttered. "Noise-making during sleep period. Inform the duty Officer so he may order the appropriate punishment."

Francesa bowed her head silently, then brought her right hand up to touch her forehead. "Aye."

"Go away." Garvis turned to settle under his blankets.

Francesa snarled at his back, knowing the man wouldn't move

again until the fire had warmed the room. Then she left as silently as possible.

Officer Varasan was lingering over breakfast when Francesa found him. One look at her expression and he sighed heavily. "Now what?"

Francesa stood before him, trying not to notice the crumbs on the shirt that stretched over his belly. Her stomach threatened to rumble, something she tried to silence with every fiber of her being. On those few occasions when she and her like were granted good bread, their sunken stomachs offered no purchase for any crumb. "I made a sound, Officer," she stated tonelessly. "Before call to work."

Varasan sighed again. As Officers went, he wasn't so bad, Francesa thought. But he was an Officer. "Where?"

"The chamber of the First Officer."

This time Officer Varasan flinched. "Stars, girl, couldn't you have picked a less important place?" He let out a long breath of air, a gust the warmth of which actually brushed against Francesa. "Though as you well know every place is less important than that." He toyed with a remnant of pastry, oblivious to the way Francesa couldn't avoid staring toward it. "Two lashes. After the morning Report."

Francesa's body tensed, then she nodded, once again bringing her right hand to her brow. "Two lashes. After the morning Report."

Varasan flipped his own hand into the general vicinity of his brow in response, then went back to his meal, ignoring her as she left.

She veered through the kitchen, coming to a halt near one of the cooks. The cook glanced down at her and smiled. "Francesa. What brings you here?"

"Are there any leftovers?" she asked, trying to keep the neediness from her voice.

The cook's smile turned rueful. "Before most of the Officers and Crew have even eaten? Not likely." He turned away, hesitated, then shoved something toward her. "This bit was ruined by a new apprentice. Get rid of it, will you?"

Francesa took the roll, her hands shaking. "Aye."

The cook glanced at her for a moment. "The harvest isn't too good, I hear."

Francesa nodded. "My friend Ivry works the fields." As bad as working around the Officers and Crew could be, at least most of the time Francesa was sheltered inside. Those in the fields took the brunt of the weather for their entire work shifts. "She says the weather went cold too early."

"The weather's always cold," the cook remarked gloomily, his eyes straying toward a high slit window where a small patch of pale sky could be seen. "Though it seems colder now, in truth. Will there be enough food this year?"

"I…" Francesa looked down at the roll in her hand. "I don't know."

"Not enough, maybe," the cook murmured. "Third year in a row. Not that there's ever been enough, not since I was younger than you, but it's worse lately. The Officers say the Captain's angry with us. And the Officers and Crew must be fed before workers like us. Captain's orders." He touched his brow with his right hand.

Francesa kept her face calm despite the anger that surged inside. Nodding politely, she hastened from the kitchen and wolfed down half the roll. She managed to pause after that, staring down at the bread and thinking of a little brother with a belly as thin as her own. Biting her lip, she wrapped the other half carefully in a scrap of rag and stuffed it into a nearby hiding place where it would be safe until her work shift finished.

The morning bells sounded, calling them to Report. Francesa joined a slowly growing column of workers like herself as they shuffled toward the Bridge. Once inside, she shoved her way toward the back, finally leaning against the cold stone and looking upward. Carvings rioted across the stone above, telling the story of the Wreck and the Survival, the Ordeal and the prophesized Rescue.

Francesa felt the cold reaching through the thin cloth of her shirt, sinking into her back, and forced herself to stand away from the stone wall. She'd have to do it soon, anyway.

The lower area filled with workers, some of them casting wary eyes on the members of the Watch who also entered to stand lining one side of the room, while other workers steadfastly pretended to ignore the Watch's presence. With security assured by the Watch, the members of the Crew filed in, proceeding to their seats on long benches set on a platform raised a few feet higher then the floor on which Francesa and her peers stood. Francesa rested her eyes on the seated backsides of the Crew and remembered for a moment that she'd once been able to find humor in that view.

After the Crew came most of the Officers, going to individual chairs placed in front of the Crew benches.

Then the Third Officer entered, standing and looking around to ensure everyone was ready. "Attention!" he yelled.

The Officers and Crew came to their feet, standing rigid, while the workers around Francesa shuffled into more erect postures.

First Officer Garvis Skein entered and walked slowly to the third level of the Bridge, set a few feet higher than that on which the Officers' chairs and Crew's benches rested. The third level was much smaller than the other two, bounded along the back by a semicircular shelf of stone. On the stone shelf, which had been polished smooth and shiny, were set many polished stones of various sizes and colors, their settings forming patterns on the slab of stone.

Garvis stood before the small shelf of stone, waiting until the Third Officer handed a lighted lamp to him. He waved his light over the shelf, making the flame dance and causing the polished stones to wink rhythmically in time. "All systems report errors," he intoned, then paused.

His audience chorused the reply, the Officers and Crew loudly and enthusiastically while the workers spoke the words with varying degrees of emotion. "Corrective action required."

"All systems failing!"

"Corrective action required," the reply came again.

"Our actions have failed! The Captain orders us to leave the ship!" Garvis thundered.

"Show mercy, Captain!" the audience cried.

"Rescue will come!"

This time the chorus held the note of finality. "For those who trust in the Captain!"

Garvis sat down the lamp, turning to face the crowd full on. "Those who trust in the Captain will be rescued! They will be taken up to the stars from whence we came and live in a place of plenty with the Captain just as our ancestors did. Those who do not follow will be left behind to toil in this world of pain to which our ancestors were banished for their failures to serve the Captain well."

Francesa had heard it all so many times she could have recited it in her sleep. She tuned out the droning voice of First Officer Garvis, thinking of the cold, the poor harvest and the thin bodies of those in her family. When the call to duty was made and everyone bowed their heads as Garvis intoned thanks to the Captain along with promises of obedience in all things, Francesa couldn't help wishing the Captain would send them something better than a promise of eventual rescue. After well over two hundred 'standard' years, as carefully measured and recorded by the Second Officer, she didn't see rescue coming with nearly the certainty of hunger and cold.

But she didn't say such thoughts out loud. Two lashes today would be bad enough.

First Officer Garvis eventually finished his instructions, holding up a copy of the writings with reverence. "Here are the rules, set forth by the Captain. Heed them. Always ask your Officers for what the rules say and what they mean. Do not attempt to read them yourself and spurn those who offer what they claim to be true copies. They are only seeking to mislead you. Only the copies of the rules kept on the Bridge are the true words of the Captain, and only the Officers may read those rules, by order of the Captain."

Once again everyone touched their brows, Francesa thinking as she did so of her father's disdain over the claim that no one but an Officer should read the writings. Tattered copies still existed among the workers, treasured and read by any who asked. Francesa had read them herself, finding comfort in the old words and their firm advice on how life should be lived.

The First Officer left, followed by the other Officers, then the Crew. Even as the last of the Crew left the Bridge, stern members of the Watch left their posts against the wall and began herding the workers out. "Back to your labors! Earn the mercy of the Captain by your sweat!" The workers openly grumbled before the Watch, but went as ordered.

The Report had eaten up more than an hour, granting a tedious but welcome respite from work. Unfortunately, the remaining hours of the morning saw Francesa scrubbing the stone walls of the Crew's lodgings. After a short mid-day break and a too-small food ration, Francesa was ordered to tend fires again.

The afternoon was well along before that task was handed off to another weary worker. Francesa peered through a high window at the light, judging the time left in the work day, then reluctantly headed for the quarters of the Watch. If she didn't get her lashes soon she might not get them today. She didn't particularly care if that displeased the Captain who had already banished them to this cold hell, but the displeasure of First Officer Garvis could be an ugly thing to bear. If he found out she'd avoided being punished two lashes would seem like a mercy compared to the First Officer's righteous wrath.

Francesa went across a cold passage and down the slope slightly to the dwellings of the Watch. Two members stood at their station, waiting for whatever task either Officer or Crew might demand.

Francesa walked toward the Watch station, already feeling her back muscles tensing in anticipation of the bite of the lash. As she stood before the Watch members, ready to report, something distracted them. Both turned to look further down the hill, their mouths dropping open and their eyes staring. Francesa couldn't help looking in the same direction.

She wondered if her own mouth had fallen agape. Something very large, larger even than the Bridge, was dropping gently down from the sky, shining even in the dim light of the red sun which managed its way through the ever-present cloud cover. The great object, moving silently, came to rest in the big courtyard which separated the homes of the Officers and Crew from the houses, farms and workshops of the workers.

"The Captain has come," one of the Watch members gasped. He turned to Francesa, smiling like a drunkard. "He's come to take us up!"

Francesa was still staring when the man turned and started running, down through the upper quarters and toward the round shining object as it settled onto the stone of the courtyard. Even from here, Francesa could see the heavy paving stones buckling around the edges of the huge craft.

But she didn't smile and she didn't run. Her mind full of a strange haze, Francesa veered off to recover the half-roll which she'd hidden that morning, then walked slowly toward the courtyard. There seemed no reason to run. If the Captain had truly returned, he certainly hadn't done so for her.

Most of the other workers seemed to feel the same way. As a column of Officers and Crew hurled themselves toward the strange object, crying out devotions to the Captain, the workers followed behind, moving with a sort of quiet resignation.

By the time Francesa reached a point near enough the thing to see and hear what was happening, it seemed the entire town had gathered around it. Closest were the Officers and Crew, most with faces beaming in anticipation. The Watch stood behind them, their faces both hopeful and worried. In the outermost ring stood the workers, shivering in the cold, their numbers far larger than the others, craning their necks or climbing on anything that might offer a view. Francesa scrambled up on a column marking one corner of the courtyard, putting her toward the very back but giving herself a fairly clear look over the heads of most of the crowd.

Garvis Skein stood closest to the strange object. Francesa narrowed her eyes, but couldn't tell if Garvis was really shaking with either fear or excitement.

With absolutely no warning or fanfare an opening appeared low in the side of the object. The rectangle seemed large enough to hold several people, but only two stood there. A low moan swept across the crowd as the two stepped down to the stones of the courtyard. Francesa squinted again, trying to make out details, then as the two walked forward was able to tell one was a man and the other a woman, though both were garbed in outfits which seemed impossibly wonderful to her eyes.

The two stopped before Garvis Skein, standing side by side.

Garvis raised his right hand to his brow. "The First Officer greets you in the name of the Captain!" he cried. Then, his voice holding the first note of humility Francesa had ever heard from Garvis, a humility she was sure was totally false, he spoke more quietly to the man. "Are you the Captain's image upon this world?"

The woman cleared her throat. Garvis gave her an annoyed look before focusing back on the man. "We are obedient followers of the Captain. As you know, of course," Garvis added hastily.

The man spoke with apparent care, his voice oddly accented, his eyes looking toward the woman. "If you want the captain, I can introduce you."

"He's not here?" one of the other Officers blurted.

Garvis shot an ugly glare toward the offender before smiling at the man again. "But if you are the Captain's image, or . . .or representative . . ."

The woman finally spoke, her crisp voice carrying clearly to Francesa. "If you want the captain -."

"Excuse me," Garvis interrupted with a frown. "I know you accompany the Captain's representative, but I am the Captain's First Officer. I speak to Him and to his other Officers." Garvis ended with a smile toward the man.

"The Captain's a man?" the woman asked, sounding not the least abashed by Garvis' rebuke.

A shocked murmur ran through the crowd of Officers and Crew. Garvis frowned again, deeper this time, his face reddening in a way Francesa knew all too well. "Of course the Captain is a man. It is clear that only a man can be the Captain. How could it be otherwise? The Captain we knew was a man, every First Officer chosen to speak for Him on this world has been a man, and it has been foretold that He will return. Is this a test?"

Far from appearing intimidated, the woman smiled tightly. "Perhaps it is a test." The man with her started to speak. "Oh, no, Kayl. Let this *man* tell you what he wants to say."

The man addressed as Kayl nodded at the woman's words. Francesa watched, her puzzlement growing. The man Kayl actually seemed to be deferring to the woman, though if he was an Officer or even Crew she couldn't possibly have any authority over him. And surely Kayl was an Officer. Who else could have come in such an amazing craft?

But First Officer Garvis seemed oblivious to the by-play between the man and woman. He faced the man called Kayl, his arms spread wide. "We are ready to depart with you."

Kayl's face grew wary. "You're descended from survivors from the *Verio*, right?" A murmur arose from the crowd and everyone, Francesa included, brought their right hands to their brows at the mention of the ship's Name. Kayl seemed startled, then nodded. "This is a pretty empty area of space. Ships very rarely traverse it. We're only here because the *Bellegrange* was chartered to make some observations that required the properties of this part of space. That brought us close enough to detect the distress beacon the *Verio* left orbiting your sun. But even after we report on survivors here it may be a long time before anyone comes back again since you do appear to be able to survive on this world independently."

Garvis smiled and nodded even though Francesa doubted he really understood what the man had said. "You have come and that is all that matters."

Kayl shook his head. "I have to explain. That's important because even though our ship is much bigger than the one your ancestors came here on, the *Bellegrange* still has limits on internal space and life support. As much as we'd like to, we can't take everyone," he stated with the air of someone declaring an unpleasant but unchangeable truth.

Francesa felt her heart sink as the little hope there vanished. All around her, other workers slumped in resignation, but she could see Garvis and the other Officers and Crew smiling, and see how Kayl seemed surprised by the happy reaction among that group.

Garvis spread his arms again. "It has long been known that all would not be Rescued. That only those deemed worthy would be taken up to the stars again. The worthy stand before you, those who have accepted the authority of the Captain without reservation, who believed He would return for his chosen and obedient followers."

Kayl looked around, his expression wary, then at the woman with him as if, Francesa thought, he was seeking guidance, absurd as that seemed. The woman murmured something so low that even Garvis frowned over not being able to hear. But Kayl obviously did. He gave Garvis a confident look. "We'll need whatever census data you have. Information on everyone here."

The Officers and Crew shuffled their feet, looking at each other in open surprise. Garvis also seemed to wonder at the request. "Everyone? But -."

"Everyone," Kayl repeated firmly.

Garvis couldn't hide the puzzlement he felt, then an Officer behind him said something and the First Officer's face cleared. "Another test. Of course. Whatever you ask we shall provide." He nodded, his smile fading into the first traces of uncertainty. "And then we shall be taken up?"

"Once we've reviewed your information we'll be able to proceed." Kayl smiled reassuringly. "It'll take a little while."

Garvis managed another smile in return. "We have waited long already and can surely wait longer if that is the Captain's pleasure. We are obedient to Him." Once again Garvis touched his brow, a gesture mimicked first by the Officers and Crew and then in a more ragged fashion by the workers watching from a greater distance. Then he waved his hand vigorously at the Second Officer, who ran off toward the Bridge.

Francesa watched the Second Officer go, knowing he was after the population records meticulously kept up to date and stored for safekeeping in the Bridge. Then her eyes returned to Garvis as the First Officer swept his hand around again, this time from the tone and volume of his voice addressing everyone in the courtyard. "The day of Rescue has come. The obedient faithful shall be rewarded. Members of the Watch! Pray you have enough obedience in your hearts to be among the faithful, and send the unworthy back to their labors."

The people making up the Watch turned and began shoving back the workers, yelling out commands. Francesa, far enough back to avoid their attentions for a few moments, gazed at the woman and the man Kayl, who were speaking together again. Both of those individuals seemed troubled, though by what Francesa couldn't guess. Perhaps they'd expected more worthies among the people who lived here.

An arm swept toward her as a member of the Watch aimed to dislodge Francesa from her perch. She dodged with the ease of someone who'd avoided blows all her life, scrambling down and joining the other workers as they hastened to their homes, occasionally looking back to the ship that sat like an impossible vision in the courtyard, forever out of their reach.

But once the workers had cleared the courtyard, heading down the slope toward their homes, the Watch turned back, forming a guard around the ship. Francesa joined up with some friends, but aside from the briefest of greetings none of them talked. What was there to say? Finally Francesa grinned into the silence. "At least once the First Officer leaves I'll never have to build his fires again."

A hand fell upon her shoulder, momentarily shocking her with fright, but then her father's voice came. "There's that, little lady. No stars for us, eh? Except the relief that'll come from being free of the 'worthy.'" A chuckle spread among the crowd, but it held little real humor.

Francesa's father used his hand to steer her to one side. "It'll be dark soon, and there's little sense in laboring more today. Come along. You're old enough to sit while we talk of this." They wended through the narrow byways of the workers' area until they reached a place where a cave mouth in a hill had been covered with roughly hewn stone. The door, formed of small boards hacked from the local vegetation, didn't fit its frame tightly, but was better than nothing at keeping out the weather. A moment later they were within the meeting hall, out of the bitter wind and seeking seats on the rough benches.

The room filled rapidly. Francesa ignored the smells of so many bodies, instead enjoying the warmth the crowd generated. Talking began almost at once, but after a while Francesa realized the conversations around her were going nowhere. What, really, was there to say? The judgment had come and here they sat downcast, while the Officers and Crew were doubtless dancing in the halls of the buildings around the Bridge.

Some length of time had certainly passed, for the gaps around the door showed nothing but darkness, when the aimless conversations ceased abruptly as the door opened and a woman stepped inside. Francesa watched her like the rest, able to tell even under the rough worker's cloak that she was too well fed to actually be a worker. Then the woman raised her head to return the stares and Francesa felt a shock of recognition. "The man Kayl's companion," she gasped.

Others had obviously identified the woman as well. A roar of talk arose, then faded into silence once more as the woman stepped away from the door. Francesa's father stood and walked forward to meet her, his nervousness plain to all. "You are, of course, welcome here."

The woman halted and eyed the roomful of workers. "Thank you. It wasn't too hard to manufacture a copy of your cloaks, though I see that didn't mislead anyone."

"The Watch is not here with you?" someone asked nervously.

"The Watch," the woman answered dryly, "doesn't know I walked through their ranks. My stealth gear isn't state of the art but it's more than good enough for dealing with them." She eyed the group. "I wanted to talk to someone else. Someone besides that group that kept everyone else away after we landed. You seem frightened. Why?" To Francesa, the woman's voice held the same assumption of obedience that she'd always heard in First Officer Garvis, yet without the arrogance Garvis always carried around him like a second cloak.

Francesa's father looked around helplessly, saw that no one else wanted to answer, then spoke heavily. "We know you're here to judge. I suppose you've already judged. And every one of us knows we're not worthy."

The woman from the ship cocked one questioning eyebrow at him. "You're not?"

"Please do not mock us. We are here, we are workers, because we lacked the same wholehearted obedience to the Captain that the Officers and Crew claim. We know that."

"And how does this make you unworthy?" the woman pressed.

A woman worker finally stood. "You know this! You know that all that matters is a person's acceptance of the Captain as the only true leader in everything!"

"Interesting." The woman from the ship seemed to be looking inward for a moment. "What do you base this belief on?"

The silence stretched this time, then Francesa's father beckoned to an old man. "Give her the writings you carry. I don't know the meaning of all this, but we've nothing to lose by doing as she says."

As the old man approached the woman from the ship, he touched his brow, then offered the tattered pages. The woman from the ship frowned as she took the writings, then began reading them, at first slowly, then with greater speed until she seemed to be flipping through the papers as fast as their brittleness would allow. Finally, she looked up and around the room. "These are survival rules. Guidance for people whose ships have been wrecked." The workers exchanged worried glances. "Are you telling me you've created a religion out of these?"

The old man's face worked with a series of emotions, as if he couldn't decide how he should react. "We . . . we created nothing. These are the writings. The Captain told us to follow them. *He* followed them."

The woman's frown relaxed into solemnity. "They're good rules. They haven't changed significantly since the *Verio* was lost here. But your ancestors seem to have combined them with the existing religious beliefs the survivors already had. I have no doubt Captain Santere -." The crowd gasped at the open speaking of the name, causing her to pause for just a moment. "Captain Santere," she repeated sternly, "followed the rules laid out in these documents. But he wasn't a god. Some ship captains *think* they're gods, but that's as far as it goes," she added.

Francesa's father gazed at her in open wonder. "Why haven't

you been punished for speaking His name? How can you say such things? Are you truly in the favor of the Captain?"

The woman looked cross. "This little joke has gone on far enough. I'm not in the favor of the captain. My name is Janis Balestra. I *am* the captain of the *Bellegrange*."

Silence fell across the room. Finally, Francesa's father spoke tentatively. "But . . . we've always been told, the Captain is a man."

"That's true. Captain Santere was a man."

"And all of his Officers were men. Only a man can be Captain and only a man can be First Officer and only men can be Officers."

This time the woman stared for a moment, then laughed. "Our records show that the First Officer on the *Verio* was Francesa Nalus. She was very definitely a woman."

Quiet fell again, then Francesa's father shook his head, not in denial but in obvious disbelief. "We've been told that Francesa Nalus was one of the Crew, but an unimportant one. We've been told that the First Officer was Radick Junis."

"Radick Junis?" the woman questioned, then seemed to be talking to herself for a moment. She laughed again. "Junis was Fourth Officer on the *Verio*. Not even the third in line to command. The fourth. Yet somehow he managed to get the real First Officer written out of her place in history and stuck himself in there. Apparently he was a much better politician than he was an officer. The Fifth Officer was a woman, too. I guess she got written out of history as well." She folded her arms, staring around the room defiantly. "As I told you, I'm Captain Balestra of the *Bellegrange*."

Francesa couldn't help herself. Her whisper sounded clearly in the once-again silent room. "Then *you* decide who goes and who stays."

Captain Balestra frowned down at her, then slowly smiled. "Yes. As Mr. Kayl told your, uh, 'First Officer' back at the landing shuttle, we can't take everyone." A sigh seemed to pass over the group. "I don't know what your expectations are, but as Mr. Kayl stated the

Bellegrange is much larger than the *Verio* was. We can carry most of the people in this accidental colony. But not everyone."

"Most?" the old man questioned. "Not a few? Not some? Most?"

"Yes. Mr. Kayl is going over the lists provided right now to determine your current population and match that to our capacity."

The worker woman's face reflected a sudden hope. "Then, after you've taken the Officers and Crew, it may be that some of us will also be taken up with you?"

Captain Balestra scowled. "Why does everyone assume these so-called Officers and Crew will get any priority? The criteria used to chose who goes is up to me. I'm not supposed to make value judgments, but that's my call."

The old man shook his head. "But they are obedient. They have accepted the authority of the Captain without reservation. The writings say -."

"These writings," Captain Balestra snapped, her anger clear, "say due respect should be given to those in legitimate positions of authority and their orders should be obeyed as long as those orders are lawful. Have you actually *read* these survival rules? They're not about just being obedient. These rules tell you to look out for each other, to share resources, to work for the mutual good so as many as possible can survive."

Francesa's father, with a courage Francesa would never have suspected, stepped between Captain Balestra and the old man. "Please. Don't harm him. We know the writings say that. That's why we're here instead of being among the chosen. Because we didn't think giving obedience to the Captain was all that mattered, or even the most important thing in the writings. Because we'd help a sick neighbor even on the Day of Rest, or break the rules if following them seemed to lead to an injustice. The First Officer, all of the Officers and Crew, say such things are wrong because the Captain demands our obedience no matter what. If you mean to punish us for our actions, then so be it. We've only lived as seemed right, by the words in the writings. But don't harm this one. He says only what he was taught by those who live on the hill."

Captain Balestra stared at Francesa's father, her anger visibly fading. "I see. You have nothing to fear from me, sir. Not you and not this man, nor anyone here." She gestured. "You're thin. You're all thin."

"Yes. The harvests have not been good. Not for years."

"You're to be credited for getting any harvests out of this land." Balestra jerked her head toward the door, indicating the outside. "This is a lousy planet. The best option you had in this system, but only an equatorial location like this has a chance of livable temperatures on a world suffering through a centuries long winter caused by meteor impact. Do you ever see the stars or are the clouds always in the way? And I assume there's no large animal or marine life to speak of?" A few workers nodded. "Died in the immediate aftermath, no doubt. And now, after a slight warming cycle caused by this world's slow axial variation, it's going to get a little colder. If my ship hadn't come by, I'd guess half of the people here would've starved to death in the next several years." A scowl appeared on her face again. "That First Officer didn't appear to have lacked for food."

"They get all they want," Francesa said. Alarmed faces turned her way, but she kept talking, long-held resentment causing the words to pour out of her. "Because they're worthy. Because the Captain says the Officers and Crew have to get priority in everything. Food. And houses. And coal for their heaters and the best clothing. And we have to serve them."

Captain Balestra looked at Francesa for a moment before speaking. "The Captain says this, does he?"

"Yes." Francesa felt something else swell up inside and blurted it out. "That's what the First Officer *claims*."

The silence in the room somehow conveyed shock. Captain Balestra gazed around, then focused back on Francesa. "That big building up the hill, the one with all the carving on it. Is that where the Officers live?"

Francesa nodded. "I work there."

"And you, and everyone here, lives in places like this?"

The old man's voice sounded ragged, as if the blasphemies being uttered were overwhelming him. "The Captain and His servants need places whose glory reflects His own glory, places where His works are seen -."

Captain Balestra slammed a palm onto the nearest table, causing everyone to jerk and the old man's words to cease as if they'd been cut off. "If you truly believe this Captain is some sort of deity then he wouldn't need anything from you to make him more glorious. As for his works, look around you! Every single one of you is a greater wonder and monument than any building could ever hope to be! Have you forgotten that?" She calmed herself, shaking her head. "It wouldn't be the first time, I guess. And it won't be the last, I'm sure."

Francesa's father was shaking his head as well. "I don't understand."

Captain Balestra nodded. "I'm sure it's hard for you all to grasp. Let's keep it simple. By rough estimate, I can take about three quarters of the population here back to civilization. Maybe a little more. As captain of the *Bellegrange* I am required to make the decision as to who goes and who stays. I need you to tell me everything that might help me make those decisions." She smiled down at Francesa. "This one at least isn't afraid to speak truth to power. And she doesn't seem upset to see me."

Francesa couldn't help smiling back. "Your arrival meant the Watch forgot to give me the two lashes Officer Varasan ordered this morning."

"Lashes?" Captain Balestra's smile slowly went away and she looked at Francesa's father, who nodded.

"For breaking rules," he explained.

"I see." Captain Balestra's voice seemed colder than the wind outside. "Do the Officers and Crew ever get lashes?"

"No." Francesa's father spat out his reply. "Everything they do is what the Captain orders, they say. So they can't break any rule or regulation unless the Captain has told them to do so. They can't be lashed for being obedient to the Captain, can they?"

"No, of course not," Captain Balestra agreed in a tone which belied her words. "I need some representatives to talk to. Five of you. You're one," she announced, pointing to Francesa's father. "The rest of you pick four more and make it quick. I have a lot more questions I need answered."

Her father turned to Francesa. "Go home. Tell your mother what's happening. She had to stay with your brother. All of you wait there for me."

"But -," Francesa started to argue.

The woman from the ship held up one hand to silence her. "This is your father? Listen to him. Captain's orders," she added dryly.

Francesa was out the door before she realized the lady captain might have been making a joke with her last statement.

Despite her excitement, once Francesa had described events to her mother and given the half-roll to her brother the fatigue of the day began overwhelming her. She wedged herself in an upright sitting position, determined to stay awake until her father got home, somehow sure he would be home, but at some point simply passed out from weariness.

She was awakened by a familiar hand on her shoulder. "Come," her father urged. Francesa blinked, trying to come fully awake, barely making out in the dimness of the room her mother already standing and holding her brother. "Your cloak. Anything you don't want to leave. Get it quickly."

Francesa wobbled to her feet, hesitated, then pulled her old ragged doll from the thin blanket which served as her bed. She swept on the cloak, then looked at her father, unable to read his expression in the dark. "Where are we going?"

"You'll see." Her father hustled them out and they began

hastening up the slope. As they went, other workers and families joined them, until they were part of a column of people.

As they entered the courtyard Francesa gasped to see members of the Watch sprawled around the edge of the space. Her father made a shushing noise. "Don't worry. Captain Balestra said she would put them to sleep. They haven't been harmed."

Francesa kept staring at the Watch members' bodies as they walked on, wanting to see the movements that would mark them as sleeping and not dead. When she finally felt sure of that and looked forward again, the star craft loomed over them. Her mind suddenly numb, Francesa kept walking, following her mother into the rectangle she'd seen earlier, stepping over the high edge and into a room where colored lights winked at points on one of the walls just as the polished stones did on the altar in the Bridge.

Her father said something to her mother, urging her onward through another, smaller opening, then took Francesa's arm. "The lady wants me here. You should stay as well."

Francesa came along as her father led her to the side of the room, where Captain Balestra stood watching the stream of workers enter. Balestra acknowledged their presence with a smile to Francesa and a nod to her father, then went back to watching, occasionally directing Francesa's father to keep the column of people moving as briskly as possible.

The line of workers finally stopped as more than a dozen men and women Francesa knew as friends of her father came in. "That's everyone," one announced.

"You're certain?" Captain Balestra questioned, then frowned at something in her hand. "Ship systems logged a number coming aboard that equals the totals given the census data we were provided."

"We never lied to the census," Francesa's father assured her.

"And my ship systems are reporting no signs of human life down hill from this location. Good. We can take twenty more, if their mass averages the same as your people."

"Watch member Yeli is a good man," one of the others offered.

Francesa's father nodded. "He's not like the others. And Watch member Tenal has a good woman for a wife. For her sake, he and his family could come."

"Fair enough. I need them and anyone else, up to twenty bodies, as fast as possible if they're to come at all," Captain Balestra directed. "Can you bring them here without rousing the rest?"

"I don't know." Francesa's father hesitated. "If the wrong people are awake . . ."

Instead of directly replying, Captain Balestra seemed to mumble something to herself for a moment. "I've used my lander's security systems to knock out everyone up hill from this spot. Take enough people to drag your friends. Now get going. Fast. And remember. Only twenty."

Francesa's father pushed her against the wall with a gesture to stay as he rushed away with the others. Francesa stood there, rigid, still unable to grasp what was happening.

Captain Balestra murmured some more to herself as if she were talking to someone else, then smiled at Francesa. "I see you brought a friend."

Francesa stared down at the doll clutched in one hand, feeling heat in her face, and shoved the doll behind her. "I'm not . . .that is . . ."

"Nothing to be ashamed of, girl. We all need things that bring us comfort." Balestra stared out the opening at the world beyond. "Especially in places like this. It's not a bad thing, unless what brings you comfort comes at the cost of other people. You hang on to that friend of yours, so you never forget this place and why you and your family are leaving it while others must stay."

Francesa gazed up at her. "Why are *we* leaving? I thought -."

"You're leaving because you were still following the survival rules to the best of your ability. That's the justification I used. Those who tried to change those rules to benefit themselves, or because they thought themselves better than you, won't be coming."

Francesa was still thinking about that when her father returned with the others, dragging or carrying unconscious bodies with them. "Twenty-one," her father gasped as he entered, three children in his arms. "There was another child -."

Captain Balestra raised that commanding hand, frowning. "Wait." She paused, as if listening. "The children are small enough. We can take twenty-one. Now, get back from the hatch. The opening, that is."

Everyone crowded away, then the walls around the opening flowed together and sealed into a solid surface. Captain Balestra murmured to herself some more, then looked up at the workers around her. "We're lifting. Don't worry. You won't feel it. It'll take about an hour to reach the *Bellegrange*. Accommodations will be tight, and food rationed, but we should be okay until we reach port and the Sanctuary people can take charge of you."

Francesa's father laughed. "We're accustomed to small homes and little food. But hope is something we'll have to get used to." He glanced at Francesa, showing surprise at her somber expression. "What's the matter? Surely you're not sorry to leave."

"No," Francesa protested. "It's just . . . what will they be thinking? The Officers and Crew, who were so sure they would be taken up. Instead, they're the ones left behind."

Captain Balestra gave her a grim smile. "You've got a good heart to still care about that. I left them what supplies and survival equipment I could spare, and I left them a message to think about. I told them I had an obligation to take those most in need, an obligation they should understand since the writings they revered urged that behavior. I told them those left would have to work hard to survive the coming colder period, but that since they'd proven very good at looking out for their own interests they should be well suited for the task. And I told them that anyone who believes in a powerful divinity who rules them perhaps shouldn't go around making decisions for that divinity, such as who is worthy and who is not."

Francesa nodded slowly, thinking of how hard life would be for those remaining behind. "But they followed the writings. You told us the writings said good things."

Balestra nodded as well. "The writings, the survival rules, do say many good things. If the so-called chosen ones had spent more time and effort actually following the letter and spirit of those rules, and less time and effort oppressing those who read the rules differently, I would've had a much harder time choosing who to leave."

Francesa's father stared downward. "So, they *were* judged."

"I guess so." Balestra shrugged. "But then, sooner or later we all are, aren't we? The important thing to remember is that we never get to judge ourselves. Come on, girl. I want to show you the stars."

AUTHOR'S NOTE
ODYSSEUS

The third story I ever sold. At the time I wrote *Odysseus*, the wreck of the Titanic had been found in the dark, frigid depths of the Atlantic ocean. Like everyone else, I viewed the pictures of the wreck and found them fascinating. But I'm also a sailor, and I couldn't help thinking of all who had died on that ship, of the many who had gone all the way to the bottom with her. Their bodies were gone, literally dissolved into the waters in which they lay, but still this was their resting place. And then expeditions began recovering items from the wreck, bringing up souvenirs. That just felt wrong to me. The result was *Odysseus*. A spacecraft faces a physical and a moral dilemma when it stumbles across a legendary wreck. The law says one thing, the desire to profit says another. But just maybe the original crew still has a say in the matter.

ODYSSEUS

It was an accident, really, an accident so improbable as to be within a hair's-breadth of impossible. Yet, every individual human life is the sum of similar vast improbabilities, so the accident may have had a certain cosmic inevitability about it. I don't know. I drive ships for a living, and leave Big Questions to the priests, philosophers and physicists.

My Chief Engineer, Val Steiner, triggered this particular accident. "The primary Umbari Coil's drifted slightly out of alignment. We need to drop out of U-Space long enough to recalibrate."

I shrugged in reply. As decisions by a ship's Captain go, this was an easy one. "If we gotta, we gotta. How long will it take?"

"Half-a-day. Maybe."

"Maybe?" I signaled annoyance with an aggravated frown.

Steiner just smiled, secure on her pillar as god of the machinery that made my ship work. "If there's no complications."

"And if there are?"

"It'll take longer."

One of my passengers happened to be present, and now he leaned forward, frowning as well, though in a questioning way. "Excuse me, Captain. Why is this a problem? Doesn't your ship have a back-up Coil?"

I smiled reassuringly back at him. "Sure, Mister Garand. That's the rule. Every ship is required to have two fully functioning Umbari Coils running. That's why we have to recalibrate the primary one. If it drifts far enough out of alignment to fail, or if we can't calibrate it, we just pop in a replacement Coil immediately. No big deal."

"But we have to drop out of U-space?" Garand didn't seem particularly reassured. "We're not in distress, are we?"

Val shot him her own confident grin. "Of course not. And once we've recalibrated the primary Coil, we'll be sure we won't be in distress anytime soon. Just a little preventive maintenance, that's all." Garand nodded and left the bridge, still looking somewhat uncertain.

"Thanks for not mentioning the failure rate of Umbari Coils. That might have scared the passengers," I mockingly praised Val.

She sketched a sarcastic salute with her right hand in reply. "No problem, Captain. Besides, my Coils don't fail."

"Sure. That's why we've got two working constantly." I triggered the all-hands circuit to warn we were dropping out of U-space, waited several minutes to give everyone a chance to strap down, then initiated the sequence. The world swam off-balance/inside-out for a moment, then the screens cleared to reveal the black emptiness of interstellar space. A trillion stars stared down coldly, their light magnificent but frightening, like distant fires mocking someone drowning in a sea vacant of everything but the certainty of lonely death.

Or it should have been vacant. Instead, Victoria Watabayashi, my First Officer, turned to me with an expression of amazement. "I'm picking up a ship's beacon."

"You're kidding."

"Nope." Wata adjusted her controls, fingers dancing across the panel as if she were a pianist. "The signal's really strong, boss. We're almost on top of it."

"Jesus. Another ship in normal space between stars and we dropped out into its lap. What are the odds of that?"

"Beats me." Wata's fingers played another brief tune. "Strange. I can't ID the beacon. It's not in the current ships' registry."

"So check every reference we've got. If it's in space, one of those should have it."

"Doing it now." She smiled. "Got it. Registry is..." Wata's face paled as her smile vanished.

"What's the matter?" I keyed my own panel to view the readout, then froze in turn. "*Odysseus?*" I finally whispered.

"*Odysseus,*" Wata confirmed in a shaky voice.

* * *

My ship's mess deck didn't fit anyone's definition of spacious, but it did encompass barely enough room for my few crew members and even fewer passengers to all gather together. The crew, experienced enough to know such a meeting while underway was extremely unusual, stared at me with a mixture of misgiving and curiosity, while the passengers idly waited in blissful ignorance. "Okay, everybody, we've encountered another ship." My crew's wonderment visibly intensified, in counterpart to the calm acceptance of the news by the passengers. "Not just any ship. It's the *Odysseus.*"

It took a moment for every member of the crew to realize the significance. The reaction was palpable enough for even the passengers to notice this time. One of those passengers, a physician named Ortega, pointed a blunt finger my way. "What does that mean? What is special about this other ship named *Odysseus?*"

Val answered before I could. "*Odysseus* was the first," she advised. "The first manned ship outfitted with a prototype Umbari Coil, the first ship sent off to another star. The same star, as a matter of fact, that we're heading for."

"I see. Did it reach the star?"

"No one knew, until now. *Odysseus* jumped into U-space, and vanished. Nobody has ever known what happened to her, but there's been speculation that she was doomed when her Umbari Coil failed. She only had one."

"Only one?" Garand wondered. "You confirmed to me earlier that every ship now has to have two. Why did they only have one?"

"They thought one was enough," Val stated curtly. "They were wrong."

"The fact that we've found *Odysseus*," I added, "tends to confirm that theory. We're closing on the derelict, and so far we haven't seen any obvious external damage. It's still on course for its destination, though it won't get there for more than another century yet at the speed it's making in normal space."

"Derelict?" Doctor Ortega questioned. "This means the crew is dead?"

"It's been almost two hundred years," Val pointed out. "There's not a ship made which can sustain a closed environment that long, even when everything is working, and Umbari Coils tend to drag other equipment down when they fail. Most likely, the crew's been dead for almost the entire time."

Silence reigned for a moment, then somebody whispered the word I knew would come up sooner or later: "Salvage."

"Yeah," I immediately agreed, before a dozen disparate conversations could spring up on their own. "The *Odysseus* is derelict, long-abandoned. Whoever finds her can claim the ship and everything on her."

"Christ, Captain, this isn't just any derelict. It's gotta be worth a fortune."

"Yeah," I agreed again. "A very large fortune. Under salvage law, a portion of that fortune would go to everyone aboard this ship. The question is, what do we do about it?"

"What do you mean?" a passenger demanded. "If its worth that much money, claim it!"

"It's not just a hunk of metal," Val replied, her voice deceptively mild. "That is, or was, another ship. A ship whose crew is still aboard, though doubtless long dead. If we board, even just to rig a tow line, it'll be the moral equivalent of digging up gold in a cemetery."

"That's stating it a little strongly," I suggested. "But that is essentially the question. Do we desecrate the final resting place of some of mankind's greatest heroes, those humans who first reached for the stars?"

"I'm against it," Cargo Master Walker declared bluntly. "Leave them alone."

"Are you mad?" Garand blurted. "That derelict is ours for the taking, and worth a fortune to us all!"

"I don't care." Walker glared around, finally centering his anger on the space somewhere between me and Garand. "My family has been sailors for generations, on the seas of Earth. Let me tell you, there's a hard and fast rule sailors follow. Leave the dead to the sea. No ship, no sailor, ever prospered by disturbing those drowned. It's not right. Let them sleep. I've no wish to awaken their spirits to torment this ship."

A hush fell across the room, the quiet finally broken by Garand's harsh laughter. "Well, I guess science has spoken! Is anyone going to let rank superstition keep them from fame and fortune?"

"That's enough," I rebuked Garand, my tone bringing a flush to his face. "Does anyone else object to boarding the *Odysseus*?"

"I do," Val announced firmly.

"You agree with Walker?"

"No. Yes." Val's mouth worked, then tightened into a thin line. "Those people, the crew of the *Odysseus*, that's their tomb. They shouldn't be disturbed, not because we fear them, but because we respect them. We owe them that."

"You said they've been dead a long time," Doctor Ortega observed.

"Not long enough!" Val shot back, then subsided, embarrassed. "Sorry."

"No problem," I stated softly. "Who was it?"

"My great-grandfather. He served in engineering on the

Odysseus." Val's eyes, icy with anger, fixed on Garand. "His final resting place deserves to be respected," she repeated.

Doctor Ortega cleared her throat, then spoke softly. "I understand your concern, as well as that of Mr. Walker, but this is far from the first ship to be found after being lost. There was that ship long ago, on one of Earth's oceans, what was the name? The Titanic. I read once there was considerable debate on whether the wreck should be disturbed or left as a monument, yet eventually some of the remnants were recovered. Is this not the same thing?"

"No." My flat response drew a raised eyebrow from Ortega. "Wrecks in deep water are different, Doctor. Unless you get to them pretty fast, there aren't any bodies left to desecrate. Everything, flesh and skeleton, disappears pretty quickly in the ocean environment. There weren't any dead left at the site of the Titanic when it was found, except in spirit. But a space wreck leaves everything behind, frozen for effective eternity. We checked the records, and no manned wreck has ever been lost for anything near this long. It's a unique case."

"Besides which," Val added sharply, "military wrecks have always been labeled national war memorials. People never hauled up pieces of sunken military ships because if they had they would have been tossed into jail."

"Was *Odysseus* military?" somebody wondered.

"It had some military personnel on board," Val confirmed.

"That's not the same thing," Garand insisted stubbornly.

"No, it's not." I nodded toward Wata. "Our records indicate *Odysseus* was officially listed as non-military, a peaceful probe of the stars. If it had been government property, we'd still have to worry about an official claim, but public sentiment of the time was such that it was funded by a quasi-private organization. Legally, *Odysseus* is private property, and thus liable to salvage. Since the derelict is still in interstellar space, no other private or governmental authority can dispute possession the way they could if *Odysseus* was in their territory."

Walker jabbed a finger toward me. "So what do you think, Captain? Your vote is the only one that really counts."

"True enough. To be honest, I don't think I want to be remembered as a grave robber, but at the same time I know that our contact with the *Odysseus* has been automatically entered in our ship's official log. I can't tamper with that log, so as soon as we reach port a lot of other people will know where *Odysseus* can be found. That'll make it just a matter of time until someone else boards her."

"At least your conscience would be clear," Val stated, with an steely glance toward Garand.

"But what if there's survivors?" Wata wondered.

"Survivors?" Every eye shifted away from me and toward Wata.

"Impossible," Val declared flatly.

"No, not impossible," Wata insisted. "Very unlikely, but if enough crew sacrificed themselves, if everything went right, there might be. We can't rule it out, that one or two descendants of the original crew might have managed to survive this long. We can't leave, not without checking to see if someone is there."

"I'm not sure I'd want to find a survivor," Walker suggested with a shudder. "Alone out here all their lives, with all the things they'd have had to do to survive?"

"They might not be exactly sane," Wata agreed. "But that's not the issue." She turned to me. "Besides, Captain, if we claim *Odysseus* we can ensure she and her crew's remains are treated properly. True grave robbers might just rip everything apart and sell it to the highest bidders."

I thought about it for a moment, keenly aware of the eyes fixed on me. "Okay. Wata's right. We do have a responsibility to check out the ship. Beyond that, I reserve the right to leave *Odysseus* in peace or place a claim and take her in tow."

Garand glared at me. "I don't think I care for that. What's wrong with a vote now?"

"The Captain just voted," Val replied with a wolfish grin, "and that's the law out here, Mister Garand."

* * *

Doctor Ortega struggled with the seals on her suit, finally getting the last one secured. "You ever been on a walk, Doctor?" I asked.

"No, not in space. I trust that is not too great a problem."

"It means you have no bad lessons to unlearn," I assured her. "There's only three hard-and-fast rules on a walk out here. Number One, anytime you're outside, make sure you're fastened securely to something. Number Two, always make sure everyone else knows where you are and what you're doing. Number Three, keep your eyes fixed on the *Odysseus* or our own ship. Don't look away."

She nodded judiciously. "I understand the reasoning behind the first two rules, but why the third? Are not the stars glorious in interstellar space?"

"They are," Val replied in a dry tone. "Doc, humans have a well-developed fear of falling. Near a planet, that's not a problem, because there's something big nearby to fall on and that makes our hind-brains happy. Out here, there's nothing, just the one-and-only bottomless pit to fall through until the crack of doom. People lose their minds staring into it, because there's nothing for those minds to hold onto. Keep your eyes on the ships."

"I will," Ortega promised, paling slightly. She moved toward the airlock hatch, peering at an adjacent view-screen centered on the nearby hull of the *Odysseus*.

I took advantage of the doctor's preoccupation to sidle close to my Chief Engineer. "Val, are you sure you want to go?" I asked quietly.

"My great-grandfather's over there, Captain. Besides, you'll need a good engineer to look at the condition of the ship."

"It's not the condition of the ship I'm worried about. Look, the crew of the *Odysseus* were lost in the middle of nowhere. The emptiness out here can eat at healthy minds in working ships, and the people on *Odysseus* knew rescue was impossible. God only knows what might have happened."

"You don't think they died heroically?"

"I don't know. I don't know what we'll find over there. Frankly, I wish someone else was going to see. Maybe they're all sitting at their posts, after working until the end. But it could be very bad. Can you handle that if it is?"

"Captain, contrary to Walker's beliefs, I don't think the dead can hurt us. The only thing we need to fear is what's within ourselves. I'm not afraid of what we might find."

"Good enough." I double-checked my own seals, then led the way into the airlock. "Okay," I announced over our suit circuit as the inner hatch cycled closed, "we can see an access hatch on the outside of *Odysseus*. Wata's maneuvered our ship so our own airlock is opposite it. We should have a straight shot." The outer hatch popped softly, revealing *Odysseus'* hull stretching from right to left across our field of vision, framed on top and bottom by strips of black spangled with brilliant stars. Clearly visible against the still-bright hull of the other ship was a large rectangle which should mark the access. I fired a grapnel across, watching as it locked onto the other ship next to the access, then led the way hand-over-hand. I reached one hand out, tentatively, my suited fingers finally brushing against the metal of a ship out of legend.

"Unbelievable," Val whispered. I turned and saw she was also gazing at the *Odysseus* with something born of disbelief and wonder. A moment later, she tore her eyes away to focus on the nearest portion of the hull. "This looks like the control panel," she noted, prying at a half-meter square panel. It resisted her efforts, frozen by time and space, until a tool forced it open.

"Will that still work?" I wondered.

Val grinned, though with tension, not humor, as she punched a series of buttons. "If not, I'll run a power cable from our ship. It looks operational, though." After a moment, I felt a lurch through the *Odysseus*' hull, followed by the smooth opening of the access hatch. "Bingo, Captain."

"Thanks." I led the way again, fighting down a feeling of intruding where I shouldn't be. The clean technology of the airlock clashed incongruously with my mental vision of penetrating an ancient burial mound. Val and Doctor Ortega hung close to me as the outer hatch sealed and the airlock began compressing. My right hand swung down to caress the holster where my sidearm rested, a rarely-used weapon usually safely sealed in the ship's safe, intended more for show than action. Memory of Wata's speculation of a survivor, and what condition such a survivor's mind might be in, moved me to free the seals on the holster. My hand closed on the weapon's grip as the inner hatch swung open with a soft sigh audible on our exterior mikes.

I'd prepared myself for a variety of sights when the interior hatch swung open, but none matched what met my eyes. An immaculate, empty passageway ran off in two directions, its dimensions obvious in the low illumination provided by glowing light fixtures at regular intervals. Occasionally, a dimmer gap showed where a fixture had failed, but otherwise the inside of the *Odysseus* seemed ready for inspection.

"There's still plenty of power." I didn't attempt to hide my surprise.

Val jerked her head to indicate aft. "They outfitted this thing with enough nuclear material to provide energy for a millennium, if it's properly rationed."

"I read plenty of atmosphere."

Doctor Ortega nodded, squinting at her read-outs. "Yes, Captain. Pressure is a little below standard, but not much. Unfortunately, it has a fairly high CO_2 component and appears to be very stale."

"Stale."

"Yes. The air in this section of the *Odysseus*, at least, has not circulated for a very long time. I would not attempt to breath it. I also would not care to smell it."

"Noted. We won't try."

Ortega peered forward and aft down the passageway. "Very tidy. It appears we can rule out hysteria, panic or insanity."

"Maybe." I reached out and began to swing forward. "Let's check the bridge."

As I'd guessed, the large passageway led through a major bulkhead, then dead-ended at another. Following the cross-passage, empty of bodies or debris like its counterpart, my little boarding party soon reached a hatch with 'Bridge - Authorized Personnel Only' spelled out in the blocky text spaceships had inherited from their seagoing ancestors. My right hand nervously patted my sidearm even as my left punched the hatch access control.

It cycled open with a deliberation which suggested resentment to my heightened senses. Biting my lower lip, I leaned in, taking in the entire bridge with one glance. "Empty."

Val followed, crowding me in the access. "I thought we'd find the Captain here, for sure."

"Me, too. This is getting spooky." All the stations were clearly labeled, making it easy to single out the Command seat. "Val, can I access the Captain's Log from here?"

"Should be able to." She studied the controls for a moment, punched in some commands, scowled, punched some more, then smiled triumphantly. "There you are. Since there's atmosphere, I set it to normal sound playback. We should pick that up easily on our external mikes. What do you want to hear?"

"All of it, but that'll have to wait. Give us the last entry."

Val punched again, then waited. Moments later, the *Odysseus'* Captain spoke to us from the past. His voice was harsh, each grim detail coming in words spaced as steadily and heavily as the footfalls of someone headed for their execution. "Chief Engineer Kurosawa confirms our worst fears. Even though we had the means to fabricate a replacement Umbari Coil, the failure of the first Coil resulted in the destruction of the rest of the Trans-Light Drive mechanism, as well as numerous associated systems. The last month of effort, futile effort unfortunately, served only to prove that repair, to put it bluntly, is impossible. The power plant remains functional, and in a cruel irony *Odysseus* remains on course for our objective. Unfortunately, at the speed we are condemned to travel we will not reach that star for centuries. The same is true of any attempt to return home. Life support will not function long enough, even for a drastically reduced crew. I have called a meeting with all hands to discuss our options."

I kept waiting for several seconds after the voice stopped, sure that it would continue. "Val, where's the rest?"

"That's all there is," she confirmed. "Last entry, in full."

Doctor Ortega tried to scratch her head, flinching in surprise as her gloved hand instead rebounded off her suit helmet. "I would have expected the Captain to leave some final message. Perhaps something happened during this meeting?"

"Perhaps. Let's go."

There's a certain consistent logic to the interior layouts of most ships. Given a need to fit a certain number of spaces with a certain number of functions within a limited area, designs usually ended up following the same relatively efficient patterns. The mess deck turned up about where I thought it should be. Unfortunately, it proved as empty as everywhere else. "Where the hell are they?" I muttered angrily. "That meeting the Captain referred to had to take place here, and he didn't leave any more log entries."

"Apparently he chose not to," Val noted. "Captain, why don't we check some of the cabins?"

"I guess we have to," I agreed reluctantly. "I don't mind telling you that if we don't find anybody in those, I'm going to be really upset."

I needn't have worried. The first cabin we checked turned out to be occupied. "I never thought I'd be so happy to see dead humans."

The bodies had been mummified in the dry, sterile environment, so that peaceful expressions were still apparent. Crossed arms rested over their upper bodies, reinforcing the impression of ancient pharaohs somehow clothed in the garb of Third Millennium space explorers. Ortega leaned over to nudge a small container floating near one bunk, bringing its label into view. "Barbiturates," she announced. "A lethal dose for each, no doubt."

"Suicide," Val sighed. "Perhaps the best option left them." She fingered a sheaf of paper lying nearby, then smiled at me with humorless triumph. "Farewell message, right here."

"They wrote them out?"

"Sure," Val carefully returned the papers to their original configuration. "They had no idea how long it might be before they were found. Any automated storage media might deteriorate in the interval, especially if power failed and let radiation sleet through the ship. But paper would last a very long time in this kind of environment."

"That makes sense. I guess they thought it out beforehand."

"Exactly." Val turned to leave the cabin. "No panic. No insanity. They left this life calmly. Heroically."

"Some of them did," I agreed.

"Some of them?"

I pointed one finger toward the fourth bunk in the cabin. "Where's the other room mate?"

Val stared, her thoughts running across her face too fast to read. "Perhaps at his or her work station," she finally suggested.

"Every work station we've seen so far has been empty. But you might be right. Let's find out." We made our way from cabin to cabin, the repetitive tragedy of the vignettes within rapidly dulling our senses. Outside the last, I tried unsuccessfully to rub my neck through the helmet seal. "We're missing three bodies, people."

"Work stations," Val repeated stubbornly.

"That's a lot of territory to check, and we're going to do it really carefully."

"Why?" she snapped, then bit her lip. "Sorry, Captain."

"That's okay. I'm glad we found your great-grandfather, but it can't have been pleasant for you. Walker may be right. I don't like disturbing these people's rest."

"Then why keep looking?" Val demanded.

"Because the three missing crew might have decided to end it all at their work stations, or they might have changed their minds. Maybe tried to live, maybe went a little over the bend after a while. Or a lot. We don't know what they might have left behind."

Ortega nodded. "Like the genie in the bottle. You know, in the original story the genie begged to be released but then declared his intention of killing the one who had released it. After waiting so long for rescue, it had become consumed with hatred. This could happen to a human, lost out here with no rescue ever coming."

Val looked around slowly, eyes narrowing. "Booby-traps, maybe? A self-destruct sequence rigged to our entry?"

"Can't rule it out. Doc, is there a quicker way to find those last three than checking every compartment and maybe tripping a bomb?"

Ortega spread her hands in apology. "Alas, no, Captain, not with what we have. A building scanner might do, but such are designed to locate living people within collapsed structures, and in any event we do not have one." Her face brightened suddenly. "Wait! The crew might have been equipped with implants to monitor their health and locations during exploration activity. If so, the sick-bay may contain a panel allowing us to pinpoint them."

"Great. Let's find it."

Painted arrows beneath the ancient sign of the red cross led us to a nearby hatch. Ortega pushed confidently through, then froze in mid-push. "Captain?"

"Yeah." The side-arm was in my hand, though I had no idea what it could do against a trap set centuries before. "What is it?"

"We have found your missing crew." She slid carefully to one side so I could see within. The hand holding my useless weapon drifted unheeded as I stared.

Three bodies floated within, so thin as to be almost skeletal, long strands of white hair drifting in gentle air currents. "There's circulation in here," I suddenly realized. "Val, seal the hatch!"

Ortega moved carefully around the figures, one forefinger tracing tubes leading into shrunken limbs, then pausing to rest against one of the small cushions on the loose frameworks surrounding each body. "Silk," she announced.

"What the hell is this?" I breathed the question. "What were they doing?"

"Staying alive," Doctor Ortega stated. "You see? A slow, steady nutrient feed, waste removal tubes, and the bodies set within an environment of absolutely minimal strain. They have simply drifted here, conserving life as best any human body may given severely limited food supplies. This area, and probably only this area, received fresh oxygen and had CO_2 scrubbed from the air. They sought to maximize the duration of their life support as well." She pointed to screens positioned above each figure's head, one still flickering with constant gray static. "Even entertainment, once. Perhaps voice activated. At some point, no doubt, the isolation and inactivity still overcame their senses. It must have been a horrible experience."

"But why?" I moved closer, repelled and fascinated by the emaciated, drifting figures. "What was the point? Why die like this instead of with some degree of dignity?"

"Die?" Ortega shook her finger at me. "One, yes. But the other two still live, Captain. There is respiration. There is circulation. There is brain activity. They still live."

* * *

"So that's it. Doctor Ortega says the two crew still living can't be moved by us without killing them. Accelerating or decelerating *Odysseus* would also kill them."

My audience, crew and passengers again gathered in my ship, exchanged glances. "It sounds as if that would be a mercy," Garand noted stubbornly.

"It might be," I admitted. "It might also be murder."

"As a rule," Doctor Ortega added, "any action taken with such fragile lives must be with the aim of aiding them. Something certain to cause death instead would not be lawful. Not without their consent, and such cannot be acquired while they remain comatose."

"So we can't move the *Odysseus*," one of my crew noted, "but we can still claim it, right?"

"I guess so." I grimaced as I replied, meeting the eyes of my crew. "I'm still not sure that's the right thing to do."

"If we don't do it, someone else will," Garand stated brusquely. "You won't be preventing harm to the derelict, you'll just be giving someone with perhaps fewer scruples the chance to rape it instead."

"And you'll be robbing everyone on this ship of their share in the wealth that claiming this wreck will bring," one of my engineers noted, flinching as Val turned a withering glance on him.

"The ship and crew which found the legendary *Odysseus* will themselves be somewhat famous," Doctor Ortega observed. "That will surely translate into some degree of wealth for those so inclined to exploit that fame."

"That won't be any damn fortune," someone grumped.

"Probably not," I conceded. "In any case, I don't know what choice I have. If I don't claim *Odysseus*, someone else will."

"No, they won't." First Officer Watabayashi, standing in the entry, shook her head as everyone's attention focused on her. "Boss, I just finished checking something I suspected as soon as you found those two crew members. We can't claim the *Odysseus*, and neither we nor anyone else can loot it. Once we make our report, a government ship will come to guard it as fast as it can get here."

"Explain, Wata. What difference do two near-corpses make?"

"*Near*-corpses," she emphasized. "Don't you realize what their presence means, boss? Part of the crew of *Odysseus* is still alive, which means the ship was never abandoned, which means legally it's not a derelict."

"So who's it belong to?" Val demanded.

"I checked. The quasi-private organization which launched *Odysseus* went belly-up after the failure. Its assets were eventually all absorbed by its government. Hence, *Odysseus* belongs to that government." She bent a polite but insincere smile toward Garand. "Sorry, everybody. Legally, we have no claim, and the only money associated with *Odysseus* is whatever finder's fee the government might offer."

* * *

My cabin had precious little in the way of space, but it did have privacy and room for another chair. Wata sat strapped in there, gazing toward the bulkhead as if she could see through it and the Umbari distortion to where *Odysseus,* now far behind us, plowed with steadfast stubbornness through normal space toward her far-off destination. "What's up, boss?" she finally asked.

"I just wanted to thank you, for finding out that *Odysseus'* legal status had changed, and for telling us."

Wata smiled, shaking her head. "Thank me? Knowing is my job, and as for telling, what else was I supposed to do?"

I grinned back, mentally at peace for the first time since we'd found the lost ship. "You could have kept quiet long enough for us to pull stuff off *Odysseus*, enough 'souvenirs' to generate a small but tidy fortune on the black market."

"Wrong, boss. I couldn't have kept quiet. I have friends who've died in wrecks, just like any other sailor does. I never knew those people on *Odysseus*, but we're brothers and sisters under the skin." Her gaze switched back to the bulkhead. "I'm glad we didn't take anything off that ship."

"We took something." I waved toward my personal safe, ignoring

Wata's sudden look of surprise and disapproval. "Val picked up the last message written by her great-grandfather. It's hers. She asked me to keep it here where it'd be safe."

"Did you read it?"

"No. It's not addressed to me. I did read a couple, but not that one."

Wata hesitated, staring at me in puzzlement. "You read some?"

"Yeah. The Captain's, because I wanted to know how he handled the worst crisis any Captain can face."

"One isn't some."

"No. I also read the messages left by the ones who lived."

"So why'd they do it?" Wata shivered. "I'm going to have nightmares, boss, just thinking about what they endured."

"Then don't think about it," I advised. "It turns out they did it partly for exactly the reason they needed to; to ensure the *Odysseus* wasn't legally abandoned. I guess Earth was in the midst of a fairly laissez faire period when they left, and they figured if someone didn't try to stay alive to look out for the others then all their bodies might get carved into pieces and sold for knickknacks or something."

"Good guess."

"That wasn't the only reason, of course." My expression shifted into admiration. "They didn't want to give up short of their goal. After calculating the resources available they figured by stretching everything to the max they might just be able to keep three people alive long enough to reach that star. They'd have to live an extraordinarily long time, but with zero strain on the bodies it might happen."

Wata stared. "The Universe screwed them and they wanted to see if they could still beat it, eh? Tough bunch of sailors."

"Tough is one word for it. They wouldn't quit, even though it meant three of them had to be condemned to a living hell." I shook my head, eyes downcast. "I can't even imagine the courage it took to volunteer for that, to endure that."

Wata nodded somberly. "I'm ashamed to say that when I first heard about the survivors I thought they'd been afraid to die, that they'd tried desperately to live simply out of fear."

"Yeah, that thought crossed my mind, too. We tend to measure human courage in terms of willingness to die, forgetting that sometimes dying is the easier way out. Staying alive, despite the odds, despite the pain, is sometimes the bravest thing any human can manage."

Wata smiled wryly. "True, boss, but that kind of attitude is kind of crazy, don't you think?"

"Crazy? Yeah. No far-future historian will ever accuse Homo Sapiens of being totally rational." I thought about the eternal night and distant, unfeeling stars outside our ship's hull. "But that crazy attitude has taken our species further than we imagined possible, and it'll take us further yet." I pulled two rum rations out and offered one to Wata before hoisting my own in a toast. "So, here's to living heroes."

AUTHOR'S NOTE
ONE SMALL SPIN

This was only the second story I ever sold. I had been working at the Pentagon on my last tour in the Navy, and one of my side jobs have involved reviewing classified documents to make recommendations about whether they should be declassified. Since this was the 1990s, I saw a lot of material dating from the 1960s that was coming up on its review date. Much of that material came from the office of Secretary of Defense McNamara. I didn't have a great impression of McNamara going in, but my view of him went down a lot more as I read the papers from his office and saw how he and his aides had manipulated data and information as if positive that no one could possibly ever catch them at it. In fact, a lot of it had already come out when I was looking at those papers. During this same period, I had been watching how NASA handled questions about robotic explorers of other planets. Suppose NASA handled robotic exploration of Mars the same way that McNamara's office handled things like the F-111 aircraft program? It wouldn't have been pretty.

ONE SMALL SPIN

Cape Canaveral - NASA today announced the successful launch of ROVER I, the first robotic interplanetary probe designed to fulfill NASA's mandate to explore the Cosmos using 'smaller, faster, and cheaper' technology. ROVER I will conduct an exploration of the surface of Mars, achieving the same goals as a manned mission at a fraction of the cost.

* * *

ROVER I Landing Site, Mars - ROVER I rattled away from the pad of its lander, six wheels spinning almost effortlessly in the weak gravity, leaving small rooster-tails of fine, red dust in its wake. A video camera mounted high on the front swiveled back and forth to transmit a view of its path to observers eagerly awaiting the news on Earth. Encountering a small patch of boulders lying like carelessly abandoned playing pieces from some mighty game of Martian marbles, ROVER I consulted its navigation programming, then turned ninety degrees and surged ahead once more toward a smooth patch of sand. Hitting the smooth patch, its wheels began spinning faster, hurling greater spumes of red powder into the thin atmosphere. Pivoting, ROVER I succeeded only in digging itself deeper into the sandy depression, all six wheels now buried up to the hubs in Martian quicksand. Halting at last, it sent a plaintive query back to Earth. Working across millions of kilometers, human technicians sent commands to rock back and forth, their efforts resulting in ROVER I burying itself up to its axles in the soft, red trap.

* * *

NASA Conference, Houston -

"There must be some way to free ROVER I from that patch of dust."

"I'm afraid not, Doctor Singleton. We've tried everything, even using the sampling probes to dig in for leverage, but ROVER I just got too deeply into the fine sand to pull itself out unaided."

"Unaided? What sort of aid does it need?"

"Actually, a mild push would do the job, or a tug on an extended sampling arm."

"That doesn't do us any good."

"No, sir, but at least ROVER I can examine the portion of the Martian surface within the radius of its sampling probes."

"How large an area is that?"

"About four square meters."

* * *

Talking Points, to accompany NASA Press Release -

Q. "How would you characterize the results of the ROVER I mission?"

A. "As noted in the press release, ROVER I performed in accordance with its design parameters. The robot landing vehicle has successfully conducted an extremely in-depth examination of a limited area of the surface of Mars."

Q. "Exactly how much of the surface has ROVER I explored?"

A. "Since ROVER I continues its activities, the exact area which has been exhaustively examined is naturally in flux."

Q. "If ROVER I was such a success, why does ROVER II need to be sent?"

A. "ROVER I has only been able to examine a limited area. ROVER II, by building on the experience of ROVER I, will be able to cover a much larger portion of Mars."

* * *

Cape Canaveral - NASA announced that telemetry from the ROVER II delivery vehicle indicates a successful, soft landing on Mars. After conducting a series of self-checks, the robotic ROVER II will continue the exploration of Mars begun by ROVER I.

* * *

Mission Control, Houston -
"Oh, Geez."
"What?"
"ROVER II's High-Gain Antenna won't deploy. It seems to be stuck."
"So punch it. Try rocking it with retract and deploy commands in series."
"I did. Whatever it's snagged on won't let go. We need a few more ounces of force."
"Where are we going to get a few more ounces of force on Mars?"

* * *

NASA Conference, Houston -
"Why can't ROVER II function without the High-Gain Antenna deployed? Our space probes have been able to work using lower rate antennas as back-ups."
"Yes, Doctor Singleton, but a planetary probe is dealing with too many variables for low-gain antennas to work for control. Right now we can't tell what the attitude of ROVER II is, or get anything approaching a video feed."
"So?"
"After ROVER I got stuck, Administration insisted on positive control from Earth of all movement by ROVER II. That means we have to use the camera to identify a clear path before we transmit a movement order."

"Listen, ladies and gentlemen, there's a lot of high-level interest in making the ROVER program work, especially after all the money expended to date."

"We know that, Doctor Singleton. We think we've worked out a way to jar the High-Gain Antenna free. It should be relatively low-risk, and its our only real option."

* * *

Mission Control, Houston - Commander Stan Halstead leaned over the control console, eyeing the readout dubiously. "Let me get this straight. You guys are going to deliberately crash ROVER II into a rock?"

The console operator rolled his eyes at a companion manning the next console. "Astronauts. I thought you guys were scientists. Look, we need a couple of ounces of extra force to pop the High-Gain Antenna open, so we've identified a nearby rock formation and exactly calculated the necessary speed to achieve an impact that will deliver those ounces of force without damaging ROVER II. Piece of cake."

Halstead shrugged. "I'll take your word for it. Personally, I'd have thought the extra variables would have made the problem too hard to work from here."

"What extra variables?"

"You know, planetary gravity and terrain. If ROVER II's going uphill even a little, it'd be too slow to get enough impact, and if it's going downhill at all, it might go too fast and break something. With the High-Gain Antenna out, I'm amazed you were able to determine enough about the surrounding terrain to compensate for that."

"Uh, yeah."

* * *

Mars - Rolling sedately toward a large boulder, ROVER II hit a steep slope four meters short of the target. Accelerating wildly, the probe struck the rock violently. The High-Gain Antenna popped free, whipping forward and slamming against the video-camera mount, which shorted out in a flurry of sparks. With debris from the shattered antenna lying across the power bus, ROVER II's power cells overloaded and erupted into flame. Briefly, a small bonfire warmed the cold desolation of the Martian plain.

* * *

Cape Canaveral - The launch of a booster carrying ROVER III, the latest in a series of robotic planetary explorers, was celebrated by NASA today. ROVER III, following in the footsteps of the first two ROVERs, will continue the awesome exploration of another world despite some controversy over the program here on Earth.

Senator Claghan, in a testy exchange with witnesses before her subcommittee, demanded to know how cost-effective the ROVERs have been compared to a manned mission and inquired whether NASA was continuing to evaluate manned alternatives or was "fixated on the non-human option." NASA insisted that all alternatives remained on the table despite an official stance in favor of robotic exploration missions, and trumpeted the success of the robotic policy to date.

Doctor Singleton, senior NASA administrator in charge of the ROVER program, noted that the ROVER explorers have provided unprecedented information on the Red Planet. ROVER II, he noted, elicited a remarkable level of detail on the difficulties of navigating through the rugged Martian terrain despite the unexpectedly short life of its power cells. When quizzed by Senator Claghan regarding the wisdom of dropping explorers into "rugged" terrain, Doctor Singleton announced that a different landing site with more promising terrain had been selected for ROVER III.

* * *

ROVER III Landing Site, Mars - Rocks ranging in size from clenched human fists to ones that rivaled the height and width of supermarket shopping carts littered the smooth plain. Coming down gently, the probe delivery vehicle landed slightly askew, propped on one of the smaller stones. Latches retracted, allowing clamshell doors to fall open with slow dignity, a fall that was halted prematurely when one section struck against one of the larger rocks. Inside the probe, ROVER III spun its wheels impotently, unsuccessfully trying to climb out of its tiny prison.

* * *

NASA Conference, Houston -

"Only one door is stuck. Why won't the rest open?"

"Because they're all slaved together, Doctor Singleton. The idea was that the combined weight of the doors would make sure they all fell open."

"Why did we drop it into all those rocks?"

"They were too small to see from orbit. It looked like a smooth plain."

"What can we do? We need answers, people!"

"Well, there's no way to open the doors enough for it to get out, but ROVER III can see segments of the planet through gaps left by the doors when they partially opened. We think some of the sampling probes might be able to reach through the gaps and get some surface samples."

"So its not a failure, then? ROVER III can carry out its functions?"

"It can't go anywhere."

"But where it *is*, it can do everything, right?"

"Kind of like ROVER I?"

"No, not like ROVER I. This is a totally different situation. The landing vehicle suffered from a minor problem, but there's no failure on the part of ROVER III. Am I wrong?"

"No, I guess not."

* * *

Senate Hearing Room, Washington, DC -

"If ROVERs I, II, and III have been so successful, why is ROVER IV needed, Doctor Bray, and where is Doctor Singleton?"

"I'm sorry, Senator Claghan, but Doctor Singleton had to remain at the Cape for final launch preparations. Senator, like any exploratory program, each mission can only accomplish so much. Exploring the New World required more than just Columbus' first voyage, and we've got literally an entire new world to discover here. The fact that much more remains to be found is no reflection on the undeniable achievements of the earlier ROVERs."

"I'm a little vague on these 'undeniable achievements' you're citing, Doctor Bray. My staff has uncovered numerous complaints regarding the paucity of data produced by the ROVERs."

"Senator, scientists are like little children when it comes to raw data: they always want more and they always want it now. I don't believe you'll find any scientist unwilling to admit that the ROVERs have been responsible for producing unique and uniquely valuable information about Mars."

"I am willing to concede that, but must reiterate my concerns over the small amounts of that information. My staff estimates that, in toto, based on the data released to date the first three ROVER missions have conducted in-depth examination of less than ten square meters of Mars."

"Senator, I can't imagine where that figure could have come from."

"Do you have a different one?"

"I'll have to check with Houston, but I'm certain we'll be able to provide a different number. As I'm sure you are aware, ROVER III is still functioning so the amount of Mars being covered is constantly changing."

"I'd understood ROVER III is immobile, Doctor Bray."

"I don't know where you got that information, Senator. I assure you, and I'd be prepared to assert this under oath, that ROVER III's propulsive system is not now and never has been inoperative."

* * *

ROVER IV Landing Site, Mars - High in the sky, so deeply blue it hovered on the edge of black, a new light flared to life among the brilliant stars. Initially racing across the heavens, the light slowed, crawling to a halt, then began tracking in the other direction. Finally, the fiery beacon winked out, but soon afterwards another light appeared, growing in size rapidly as it hurtled toward the surface. Somewhere in the distance, the meteor struck with such force that Martian soil trembled briefly.

* * *

NASA Conference, Houston -

"What happened?"

"The retros fired on schedule, but they didn't shut down. We sent an override to make them halt, but by the time it got there their fuel had been expended. Apparently, not every retro burned out simultaneously, so the final spurts started a tumble in the probe. We can't be sure from here, but we think the result was that instead of kicking the landing vehicle into its planned trajectory, the prolonged burn ended up spinning it through the atmosphere at the wrong angle and too high a speed. The landing vehicle couldn't deploy and the whole thing hit the planet in a catastrophic impact."

"How could such a minor failure have wrecked the entire mission? Who failed here?"

"We're sorry, Doctor Singleton, but there was nothing else we could do. By the time we could see the problem and get a command back, it was too late. Even lightspeed isn't fast enough to maintain positive control of a quickly moving situation that far off."

"'Sorry' is not an acceptable response. We cannot afford another, um, limited success. Period. There's too much visibility, too many questions being asked. The next mission *must* produce a wealth of results, or large portions of NASA's interplanetary exploration budget will be on the chopping block."

"Is it time to reconsider the entire programmatic approach, then?"

"What do you mean?"

"Doctor Singleton, every problem encountered by the ROVERs to date on Mars would have been easily overcome by a human explorer on-scene. Perhaps a manned mission-"

"We are committed to the ROVER *unmanned* exploration program. Understand? NASA cannot afford the expense of a manned mission."

"But the cost of *five* robotic missions-"

"And, I might add, there is nothing human explorers could do that the ROVERs cannot. Robotic explorers carry all the scientific equipment human explorers could."

"But if the best way to explore Mars-"

"The best way to explore Mars, and every other planet in this system, was determined before the ROVER program began. Robots are faster, cheaper, and better than manned programs. Every official evaluation since then has reconfirmed that finding. I know, because my office was responsible for producing those evaluations."

"Excuse me, Doctor Singleton. They assigned the ROVER office responsibility for evaluating the success of the ROVER program?"

"Of course. Who knows more about the program than we do? Now, I want a solid proposal for a means to ensure no limited successes like those we've encountered with ROVERs I through IV."

"I told you. Send a human."

"You don't appear to be functioning as a team player. Perhaps you'd be more comfortable in the trans-URANUS probe development office. Yes, Doctor Bray?"

"There may be a way, sir, to avoid these problems without using a manned spacecraft. It's really just a matter of perspective."

* * *

NASA Conference Room, Cape Canaveral -

"I don't understand." Commander Halstead peered at the laptop computer screen with a quizzical frown, then back at Doctors Singleton and Bray. "This looks exactly like a scaled-down version of the preliminary spacecraft design for a manned mission to Mars."

Doctor Bray shook his head with a tight smile. "It's not. This is something else entirely."

"What?"

"It's a Forward-Deployable Maintenance Facility, or FODMAC for short."

"Huh?" Halstead jabbed one finger at the diagram. "Isn't that the lander?"

"No. That's an Individual Egress Module, or IEM. It's to be used only if maintenance activity on ROVER V is required."

"Maintenance on ROVER V?" Halstead questioned. "Does this mean the ship-"

"The FODMAC."

"-is going to Mars?"

Doctor Singleton frowned and wagged one finger at Halstead. "No, no, no. Nothing in the FODMAC's mission statement has to do with going to Mars. The FODMAC will simply be required to maintain necessary proximity to ROVER V to be able to conduct maintenance if essential."

Halstead let out a long breath. "Excuse me, but I take it I'm going to be the one manning the, uh, FODMAC?"

"No," Bray corrected gently. "You will be assigned to the FOD-MAC. The FODMAC is not defined as a manned vehicle."

"Even if there's a man inside?"

"Come now, Commander Halstead," Doctor Singleton chided. "Just because we work in this building doesn't make it a manned vehicle, does it?"

"Correct me if I'm wrong, but this building won't be going into orbit around Mars."

"Neither will the FODMAC," Singleton stated sharply. "An orbit is defined as the movement of a smaller body around a larger one. The FODMAC will always maintain a fixed position relative to ROVER V or its landing site. It will *not*, therefore, ever be in orbit."

Halstead leaned backward, eyes shifting from one administrator to the other. "I am, however, an astronaut. Why do you need an astronaut to 'occupy' something that isn't a ship and isn't going to Mars?"

Bray cleared his throat and smiled again. "I see you haven't read your e-mail yet today."

"My e-mail?"

"Yes, if you had, you'd know that your job classification has been officially changed. You are no longer occupying an astronaut billet. Commander Halstead, you are now an On-scene Maintenance Technician."

"I see. What if I don't want to be an On-scene whatever?"

The two Doctors exchanged glances. "In that event," Singleton advised, "you will of course be released from duty with NASA and returned to your parent military service for assignment. Naturally, the secrecy oaths you signed regarding classified mission details will remain fully effective, and any discussion of the FODMAC or your role in it will be forbidden. Alternatively, you can chose to participate, and have some role in this historic mission. The choice is yours."

* * *

Vicinity Mars -

Commander Halstead shifted uncomfortably, trying for the millionth time to fully stretch in the small compartment that had been home for months. His head jerked as the communications panel buzzed to warn of an incoming message.

"FODMAC, this is Houston. ROVER V has encountered difficulty deploying from the pad of the landing vehicle. Conduct an egress and carry out necessary maintenance."

Halstead's heart leaped. "Roger, Houston. I understand you desire I conduct a landing on Mars near the ROVER."

Long minutes passed as light waves crawled back and forth through the emptiness, before Houston's reply finally roared forth. "Negative, FODMAC! Negative! Your reply used improper and unauthorized terminology and has been purged from system records. We repeat, you are to conduct an egress using the IEM and achieve necessary proximity to ROVER V to conduct any required maintenance, then return to the FODMAC ASAP. Do you understand?"

"Yeah, Houston, I understand."

* * *

A trail of footprints marked the Martian soil, leading from the still-smoking site of the IEM touchdown to the pad where ROVER V sat like a huge, ugly stamen in the middle of a petal formed by access panels which had dropped open on every side. Halstead glared sourly down at the machine, noting that the retaining clip on the left rear quarter of the ROVER had failed to release and was holding it captive. Pulling out a long screwdriver, he bent awkwardly, inserting the tool inside the latch and tugging. The latch popped open and retracted, freeing the ROVER, which immediately surged into motion, seeming to bustle merrily away across the red landscape.

Commander Halstead trudged heavily back to the IEM, pausing at the ladder, then stared toward the glowing spot of light far above that marked Earth. "To hell with it," he muttered, then fished an oblong of stiff paper from the tool kit and smiled at it. One side of the postcard was given over to a picture of the American flag. On the blank side, Halstead had earlier written 'Kilroy was here' in large letters. Jamming the screwdriver blade through the paper next to the flag's union so that it served as a crude jackstaff, he planted the tool handle-first in the soil, then stepped back and sketched an elaborate salute. Leaving the tiny marker, he climbed back into the IEM.

* * *

NASA Press Conference, Houston - "Ladies and Gentlemen, I am pleased to announce that the robotic probe ROVER V is successfully completing every assigned task. Our knowledge of a wide area of the planet Mars is being significantly augmented with every passing hour as a result of the analytical and exploratory capabilities of ROVER V. In short, this an outstanding success for our planetary exploration program. Every person involved with the ROVER program should be immensely proud, as should every American."

"Excuse me, Doctor Singleton, but rumors persist that a manned expedition was somehow integrated with the ROVER program and played a role in this latest success. Can you comment on those rumors?"

"I do not know why this kind of irresponsible rumor-mongering continues to be given credence. This sort of innuendo has surfaced before and our comments are on record."

"Nonetheless, Doctor, can you categorically deny any manned involvement in the ROVER program?"

"Sir, every line of the ROVER mission plan, funding authorization, and mission objectives is available on-line for your review. Use any keywords you want to search through them. I can categorically state you will find no reference to a manned mission to Mars therein. Does anyone else have questions?"

"Doctor Singleton? There has been an ongoing dispute over the relative worth of manned missions versus robotic exploration, with partisans of human explorers insisting there is no substitute for human involvement given the inherent limitations of any machine and the huge distances involved in space travel. How does this success for the ROVER program affect that debate?"

"We have not been involved in any 'debate,' as you characterize it. We were assigned the mission of achieving planetary exploration quickly and at minimum cost, using robotic explorers, and we have done so."

"But, Doctor, this is the fifth ROVER mission. Counting the previous ROVERs, the time spent designing them, building them, and in transit to Mars, as well as the costs of all those missions, wouldn't a single manned mission have been both faster and cheaper?"

"I can't speculate on such issues. Our orders were to conduct robotic exploration of Mars, and we have done so. I really can't understand why the Press is trying to harp on the allegedly limited success of earlier ROVER missions instead of the positive news of ROVER V's accomplishments."

"Doctor Singleton, in light of what you've characterized as the ROVER Program's overwhelming success, is there any foreseeable need for future manned missions outside of Earth orbit?"

"I would say the official record speaks for itself in that regard."

AUTHOR'S NOTE
SECTION SEVEN

How do you hold together a society spread across the stars? The answer in many stories involves using force, but how practical might that be if you have to worry about moving enough force to control a planet across the distances between stars? At the least, it wouldn't be easy. Maybe there would be more subtle ways to keep people seeing themselves as part of a wider group rather than separate. Methods so subtle that very, very few people would even know they were being used.

SECTION SEVEN

Valentia looked beautiful from orbit, but then most planets did. Foster gave the world a weary traveler's worth of attention as the lander glided down, reflecting that from a great distance you couldn't encounter temperature extremes or rough terrain or the bites of bugs that wanted to eat you even if they couldn't digest you. Not to mention encountering the people, who were always the source of the particular problems Foster dealt with.

The customs official barely glanced at Foster's standard ID before feeding it into his desk scanner. A moment later, the ID popped back out onto the counter where he could pick it up.

"HaveanicestayonValentiaMr.Oaks," the official mumbled before reaching for the ID offered by the next traveler.

Foster retrieved his ID, took two steps past the customs desk, and found himself facing a trio of individuals wearing dark uniforms and stern faces. One of the port police officers held out her hand. "May I examine your ID, sir?"

"Uh, of course." Foster let his own expression show an appropriate level of surprise and a hint of worry as he fished out the ID again. "Is something wrong?"

The officer took the ID and slid it into a portable reader before answering. "Just a random check, Mr. Oaks. Valentia wants to make sure all travelers have good stays here. What brings you to Valentia?"

Foster smiled with the practiced enthusiasm of a sales professional. "I represent Inner Systems Simulations. You've heard of ISS?"

The officer's responding smile was both polite and brief. "No. Sorry."

"We make some of the finest entertainment software. Just in the Inner Systems right now, but we want to expand our market. If you'd like, I can show you some of our -."

"That won't be necessary." The officer removed the ID from her scanner and returned it to Foster. "Have a nice visit to Valentia, Mr. Oaks."

Foster smiled back with the same degree of professional insincerity, though his smile could've been genuine. Posing as a sales professional had numerous advantages, not the least of which was the ability to drive away questioners by beginning to offer a sales pitch. It never hurt to cut short an interview, even though his false IDs couldn't be spotted by any scanner and his cover story was solid.

Outside of the port terminal Foster squinted against the brightness of Valentia's sun. He hailed a cab by raising one hand in a gesture understood everywhere humanity had gone, directing it to the short-term rental business apartment complex where Mr. Oaks had his reservation. Foster didn't bother looking around for anyone tailing his cab, since that would have been a tip-off he thought he might be followed. Instead, he watched the scenery roll by with every appearance of boredom.

Foster checked in, went up to an apartment whose interior decoration could've placed it on any of a score of worlds, and swiftly changed clothes. The Valentian styles in his bag hadn't aroused any suspicion at Customs, since many tourists didn't want to look like tourists. A few minutes later, he was leaving the apartment complex by a different way than that he'd entered through. A brisk walk took him to a restaurant, where he paused to examine the menu in the window while also checking the reflection for anyone following him. There weren't any apparent candidates, but Foster took the precaution of checking for tails in two other restaurant or shop windows before entering an establishment promising authentic Italian cuisine using the finest native Valentian ingredients.

Like all sit-down restaurants, it had restrooms. And like most restrooms, these were located near a service entrance. Foster had no trouble leaving via that entrance, then criss-crossing further into the city before finally entering a hotel and registering there as Juan Feres using another one of his IDs. Only after reaching his room there did Foster actually unpack.

His data pad linked to the local net with some difficulty, causing Foster to frown. Once linked, he located the local classified ads and searched for the one he wanted, one advertising antique Beta videotapes for sale at prices too high for anyone to be interested. Foster called up on his data pad an ecopy of a venerable novel entitled Dykstra's War and went to the page that correlated with the Standard Federation Julian Date. The prices and titles of the Beta tapes provided coded links to words on that page, giving Foster a phone number in the city.

The phone number was answered by a recording. Foster waited until the ancient sign of the beep sounded and spoke his message. "Juan here. I'm at the Grand Frontera Hotel, Room 354. I have a message from your sister Kelly on Innisfree."

Then Foster waited. After a bit, he began wishing he'd paused long enough to pick up some of the authentic Italian/Valentian food. Room Service provided an overpriced and overcooked plate of 'authentic nachos' which in addition to chips and cheese included some sort of small fish filets and what appeared to be a raw egg cracked into the center of the plate. Foster sighed, chewed some of the latest stomach calming medicines available in the inner systems, then ate carefully around the egg, or whatever it was. Dealing with local tastes in food was just one of the occupational hazards of his job.

A soft tone announced his room had received mail. He checked the message, ensuring its enthusiastic response included the counterphrase needed to confirm it'd come from his Valentian contact. Referring to Dykstra's War again, Foster decoded the information in the reply to find an address in the city.

The local mapping system balked at working with his data pad, causing Foster to frown again. He finally got the directions he needed, saw his destination was too far to walk, and headed for the public transit system, carrying his bag along. It didn't do to leave bags unattended in hotel rooms if you could help it. Especially bags whose shielded, wafer-thin concealed compartments contained a variety of false IDs as well as other useful materials.

Sitting on the subway gave Foster a decent excuse to idly glance around. None of the other passengers seemed to be suspicious, and none left at his stop. Foster nonetheless took a circuitous route to his destination, weaving back and forth along several blocks and checking unobtrusively for tails, before finally reaching the doorway of a private residence.

A nondescript man of medium size and build answered Foster's ring. "Hello. Are you Juan?"

"That's me. Wide and free from Innisfree." Foster winced internally at the code phrase. He didn't make them up, but he had to say them.

"I wasn't sure Kelly had left Barbadan. Is she still engaged to Collin?"

Foster nodded. "Now and forever."

Sign, countersign, and counter-countersign exchanged, the man let Foster in, closing the door carefully behind them, and led the way into the house, bringing Foster to a nicely laid-out library room and closing that door as well before speaking again. "I'm Kila. Jason Kila. Welcome to Valentia."

"Gordon Foster. This room's secure?"

"Tight as a drum. No one can see or hear us."

Foster sat in the nearest chair and leaned back, relaxing for the first time since he'd arrived on Valentia. "Can you bring me up to date?"

Kila sat down as well and shrugged. "Not much has changed since my last report. Just more of the same."

"I noticed compatibility problems with the local software."

"Oh, yeah. They've got this operating system they claim is easier to use and more reliable than Federation standard, and also fully compatible. Some of the stuff in it *is* easier to use, other's harder. I don't know about the reliable part. I do know it's less and less compatible every time they tweak it."

"We'll have to take care of that."

Kila grinned, his lips drawing back to expose his back teeth. "You've got authority to act?"

Foster nodded. "Once I've heard everything. What else?"

"Here." Kila fished in one pocket, then tossed a small object at Foster. "Local ammo."

"Hmm." Foster frowned down at the bullet. "It's too small for 9mm and seems too big for 5.6mm."

"Right. Good eye. It's 6.8mm."

"Six point eight?" Foster let exasperation show. "Why the hell are they producing ammunition incompatible with Federation small arms standards?"

Kila rolled his eyes disdainfully. "They wanted one round for pistols *and* rifles. So they picked something smaller than a 9mm pistol round and bigger than a 5.6mm rifle round. They call it universal ammo."

"Universal?" Foster laughed. "They create a new ammunition type incompatible with Federation standards and then label it universal? I guess I should give Valentia credit for sheer gall."

"Yeah. Between the operating system and the ammunition, we've got a slowly accelerating gap developing between Valentia and the rest of the Federation. There's already talk about altering the mass transit gauge 'to better suit local conditions.' It's all in my report."

"What about the Federation demarches to Valentia demanding conformity to standards? Has there been anything about those in the local press? Any public debate?"

"Nope." Kila shook his head for emphasis. "The government's sitting on the demarches. There's been a few questions raised about diverging standards, but they're very isolated. Most locals don't see it as anything to worry about."

"Okay. Valentia thinks they can sit in their own little corner of the Federation and do whatever they want." Foster flipped the bullet back to Kila.

Kila snagged the shiny object and eyed Foster. "Pretty much. What do we get to do about it?"

Foster turned up the corners of his mouth in a humorless smile. "We get to mess with a few things."

"Yee-hah. When do we start?"

"Right now. Have we got a software engineer on planet?"

Kila nodded. "Of course. Janeen Yule. She's very good."

"Give her this." Foster slid open the heel of his shoe, revealing another shielded compartment, and removed a data coin. "It contains a worm called Black Clown."

"Black Clown?" Kila took the coin gingerly, turning it over between two fingers. "What's it do?"

"It makes things harder. Have Yule make any necessary changes to match it to Valentia's new operating system. Once we introduce it onto the Valentian net it'll propagate like crazy."

"The Valentian firewalls won't stop it?"

"No."

Kila clearly wanted to ask more, but simply nodded. "I'll get it to Yule. Are you sure you don't want to hand it off personally? Yule might have some questions for you."

"If she does, you pass them to me. I want to maintain tight compartmentalization of this operation. I don't need to know what Yule's local cover is."

"You're the boss." The coin disappeared into Kila's clothing. "What about the ammunition?"

"I'll need access to the fabrication module controllers in the manufacturing facilities. For the ammunition, and for the firearms the Valentians are building to use that stuff."

Kila's brow furrowed for a moment. "You'll need to work directly with one of our on-planet people for that. Not Yule. Jane Smith."

"Jane Smith?"

"Yeah." Kila grinned. "Her real name sounds like a cover name. Jane's burrowed into the Valentian bureaucracy. She can get you that access and not leave any fingerprints."

"Cool. It's good to have a friend in the bureaucracy."

Kila smiled again, then looked at Foster questioningly. "Speaking of bureaucrats, I heard that rumor again. The one about our pensions and stuff not being honored because officially we don't exist as Federation employees."

"There's no truth in that. We're covered. Every one of us has an official and totally innocuous identity within the Federation government. I've personally confirmed that. Those identities have nothing to do with our real work, but they're accruing all the benefits we're entitled to."

"All of us? Everybody in Section Seven?"

Foster frowned and held up a warning hand. "That doesn't exist," he reminded Kila in a soft voice.

Kila looked like he was trying to eat his last words. "Damn. Sorry."

"Just don't say it again."

"I won't. I never say it. I don't know why I said -."

"Said what?"

"Why I said…" Kila finally got the idea. "Nothing. So, it's a go?"

"Yes. I'll stay at the Frontera a few more days and then shift hotels. Is the number from the classified ad good for contacting you routinely?"

"Now and then. Don't worry about coming by here. It's a mixed business and residential district, so there's always lots of foot traffic. You won't stand out."

"Good location. Nice work."

Foster met Jane Smith two days later at a public park. She wore nice but not flashy business attire which made her look more professional than attractive. "Tatya Ostov. Bureau of Inspections."

"Pleased to meet you." Foster felt a data coin slide into his palm as they shook hands.

"Yes. I understand you've come from the Genese Islands to help out in my branch. I appreciate your help, Mr. Danato."

"I'm glad to be here, Ms. Ostov."

"Your first inspection is set for tomorrow. Please report in to the Bureau front desk first thing in the morning. I'll go over your schedule then."

"Thank you." Smith/Ostov left, and Foster made his way to the next-closest library to pop the coin into his data pad. It contained all the information he needed to memorize about his role as Julio Danato, facilities inspector from the isolated Genese Island chain brought in temporarily to help eliminate an inspection backlog at the bureau.

Foster appeared at the Inspection Bureau the next morning, where the security guard scanned his ID, then handed it back with a bored nod. Security forces on every planet fought to ensure all identification data was compiled in a single place in order to assist their investigations. That also meant only a single place had to have false information inserted in order to mislead security forces. Naturally, security forces always insisted their ID sites where hack-proof. They were always wrong.

Smith greeted Foster with cool politeness. As Ostov and Danato, they went over an intensive inspection schedule, covering a wide range of manufacturing facilities. "You need to check to make sure all equipment is operating within proper tolerances and all safety requirements are being followed," she advised. "You have authority to access any equipment and systems necessary to do that."

Foster nodded, noting as he did so the small arms and ammunition manufacturing plants buried among the other facilities he'd have to inspect. "I won't have any trouble. This a pretty extensive list, though. I may have to work late a lot of nights to complete it in the time I have."

Ostov smiled with patent insincerity. "You're a salaried employee, Mr. Danato. It comes with the territory. If you have any questions or run into any difficulties, please give me a call."

Foster started work the next day. While analyzing the list of facilities closely, he'd discovered Jane Smith had arranged it so that he'd be hitting all the places associated with arms and ammunition late in the day. He'd have to put in a special mention about her foresight once this mission was over.

Most of the facilities he inspected had nothing to do with his real task, but provided cover for the ones he needed to reach. He plowed through the Bureau of Inspections checklist at each location, grateful that the Valentians hadn't yet diverged from Federation standards on manufacturing equipment and related software.

By the time he reached the first targeted facility, the week and that day were drawing to a close. Managers eager to get on with their weekend waved him onward as Foster assured them he could conduct his checks without their having to stay late.

His work would've been considerably more difficult in early industrial days when physical jigs and forms were used to guide manufacture of parts. Instead, Foster accessed the controllers which would direct computer-guided fabrication of the parts for the new 'universal standard Viper personal sidearm.' Tolerances were tricky things. If they were adjusted just a tiny bit, everything would still look fine, and initially any test weapons would work okay, but within a short time parts wouldn't work well together. It'd take a while to figure out there was a problem, time during which manufacturers would inevitably claim operator error. If the controllers had a hidden worm cycling tolerance variances from part to part on a random basis, identifying the cause of the problem would be even more difficult.

Foster finished his work, closing it out without leaving any fingerprints within the controller software. He'd changed the master patterns and their backups, so the only way to eventually fix the Viper pistols would be to redesign them. By that time, they'd hopefully have as bad a reputation as Foster could hope for.

Another week went by, with another small arms facility and an ammunition plant included among Foster's bevy of inspection sites. His dry, routine reports were forwarded to the Bureau and buried within its data files, though not before Smith in her supervisor's job altered the identifiers on a few to make it look like someone else had inspected some of the arms facilities.

Foster was having a late lunch at a store cafeteria when he noticed an increasingly large and impatient crowd in the payment line. A heavy-set man at the front of the line was drumming his fingers on the counter as he stared at a flustered clerk trying to ring up his charge. "What's the problem? I haven't got all day."

The clerk mumbled what sounded like curses. "Excuse me, sir, I'm having trouble getting the system to accept your data."

The man glowered. "There's nothing wrong with my credit status."

"No, sir. It's just not accepting…good, there it…damn! Now it's balking at…"

He leaned over to look at her screen. "No wonder! You're using that crap the government's been pushing. Shift over to the old stuff."

"You mean the last edition of the Fed standard?" The clerk hit several buttons, waited a moment, then smiled. "It's working! Everything's fine, sir."

The customer shook his head and looked around at the others waiting in line. "That government stuff is developing more problems by the day. Didn't they bother testing it?"

Another customer nodded. "My entire office just went back to the Fed standard. It's not perfect, but at least it's not full of bugs."

A chorus of agreement sounded, but one man went against the

tide. "The government's system is made in Valentia! Aren't any of you patriotic? Don't you want to support our government against the overbearing Federation?"

The woman who'd spoken earlier laughed. "The Federation isn't messing up my work. The government is, with its worthless, bug-addled, slow, and lock-up prone system. I need software that works. That's just common sense. Or do you want to stand in line forever while the government's system chokes on ringing up your charge?"

The Valentian patriot subsided with a scowl, making no protest when his charge went through on Federation standard software.

Foster watched the little drama blandly, not showing even the smallest trace of humor when the woman declared the Federation wasn't responsible for causing the system problems at her workplace. He'd seen more and more evidence that the Valentian software system was breaking down, displaying erratic and impossible to predict failures and slowdowns. As if it had never been properly tested. Or as if a Black Clown worm spread throughout everything using that software was mutating source codes in very subtle ways.

Another month passed. All of the facilities on Julio Danato's list had been inspected, and he officially returned to the Genese Islands with a brief parting thanks from supervisor Ostov. Now Juan Feres sat in his hotel room watching the local news.

A skeptical looking woman gestured toward a video window beyond her. "Reports continue to be received of problems with the new line of universal standard ammunition and the firearms produced to use it." The video window displayed a group of uniformed soldiers with angry faces, their hands slapping at their weapons. "Our sources tell us the rifles and pistols jam more often than they work. The ammunition is prone to misfires, and will sometimes jam the weapons as well. VelArms Manufacturing and Ares Ammunition, the primary suppliers of the universal standard weapons and ammunition, insist they have uncovered no problems in the factories and suggest users are failing to employ the new weapons properly."

The video window shifted, showing a figure distorted so that neither facial features nor sex could be determined. The figure's voice was also altered, hiding it as well. "We know how to use rifles! This stuff is junk. That's all there is to it. Half the time you can't even seat a magazine of ammo properly, and when you do you can't extract it. Give the stuff time, we were told. We've given it time. It's still junk. I don't want to risk my life on a weapon that don't work. What the hell was wrong with the Federation standard weapons?"

The skeptical newscaster spoke again. "Reports have also indicated that police forces in several cities which received universal standard firearms have abandoned them and gone back to Federation standard weapons. As one officer told us, 'I won't die with a jammed gun because some idiot bureaucrat decided to fix something that wasn't broken.' We will continue following this story and report on new developments."

Another two weeks passed. Foster waited with growing impatience, which was finally rewarded during a brief visit to Kila's safehouse.

Kila grinned. "Watch this."

Another newscaster, this time a smug young man, faced the screen. "The Senate today voted to convene a special investigation into the universal standard ammunition and weapons fiasco. Hours later, the government announced that what it now characterizes as the universal standards weapons 'experiment' would be discontinued due to adverse performance issues and cost overruns."

Kila shut off the screen. "Got 'em."

Foster smiled and nodded. "I believe the operating system issue has already been resolved."

Kila flopped into a chair. "That's my assessment, too. The Valentian system now has a solid reputation as a piece of junk. Even the government has shifted back to Federation standard, because the Valentian system has gotten too buggy." He eyed Foster. "That Black Clown is one mean little devil."

Foster sat as well, feeling satisfaction rise and fighting it down. He wasn't off planet yet. The mission wasn't concluded. "You have to know you have a problem, then you have to be able to identify the cause of that problem. We created problems for the Valentians, and let them reach the wrong conclusions as to the causes."

Kila's eyes narrowed as the front-door bell rang. He opened the door and leaned into the hallway to check the doorway monitor. "It's Jane."

Foster grimaced. Coincidence, but still a bit unnerving to have three of them together here. "That's all right."

Jane showed surprise at Foster's presence, then offered a bottle filled with amber liquid. "A toast to success?"

Glasses were filled and drunk. The liquor had a fiery, exotic tang that Foster enjoyed. Not all native foodstuffs were unpleasant.

Jane sank into her own chair and looked at Foster. "This is odd, isn't it? We've won, but no one'll ever know. We sabotaged an entire planet, and we, and our superiors, are the only ones who realize it."

Foster smiled. "Sabotage is a loaded term. I prefer saying we introduced inefficiencies into non-standard elements."

"And *I'm* supposed to be playing a bureaucrat! Why is this necessary? Why couldn't the Federation have just ordered Valentia to stick to Federation standard software and small arms?"

"The Federation did send demarches," Foster pointed out. "Which were ignored. Valentia realized the Federation could scarcely afford to force a member world to conform to standards. Not openly, anyway. What Valentia didn't count on was that there are other ways than brute force to increase the price and trouble of non-conformity to Federation standards."

Kila nodded. "Even I sometimes wonder why it matters so much. If the idiots want to diverge from Fed standards, let 'em. They're the ones who'll suffer."

Foster sighed. "Initially, yes. But they wouldn't be the only ones. Certainly, the initial effects of incompatible software and changes in manufacturing standards will be felt on the world which has more trouble and thus more expense in trade, as well as less market for its goods. Long-term, though, uniform standards are what hold political entities together. Humans love to innovate, to change. Once planets started diverging from uniform standards for software, manufacturing, and everything else, the process would just keep accelerating. That'd mean growing economic and social misalignment between worlds. Growing barriers to trade, exchange of ideas, travel, and so on. Eventually, that'd mean -."

"No more Federation," Jane finished. "You'd think people would know better. Just trying to introduce new standards here cost Valentia loads of money and effort, even if it had all worked."

Foster smiled again. "If people behaved rationally all the time, they wouldn't be people. And we wouldn't have the jobs we do."

"True. Never-ending jobs, from all I hear. Where are you going to next? Another assignment?"

Foster smiled with one corner of his mouth. "If it was, I couldn't tell you. But I've got some vacation time built up. I'm going home for a little while."

"Great. Where's that?"

Foster met the inquiry with another twist of his lip.

Jane looked embarrassed. "Sorry. I just meant to be polite."

"That's okay. You understand there's a lot of things we can't discuss, even among each other, just in case someone's cover gets blown."

Kila gave one of his fierce grins. "You mean things like, is Gordon Foster your real name?"

Foster smiled again. "Are you two really Jane Smith and Jason Kila?"

They all laughed, but none of them answered the question. Foster sometimes wondered if Section Seven was really the far-beyond top secret title of his organization, or if Section Seven was itself merely a code name for some more heavily classified designation kept even from him. Wheels within wheels, and it usually didn't make sense to try figuring out where if anywhere it all ended. If people knew Section Seven existed, what Section Seven did, it couldn't function anymore, and the Federation would slowly start coming apart. Foster didn't see any good reason not to accept things as they were.

Foster made his final goodbyes and left. He altered his way back to Juan Feres' latest temporary lodging, checked out, then returned as Mr. Oaks to the short-term rental apartment. He plugged in his data port, watching as it seamlessly matched the Federation standard operating system now being employed by the rental agency. Foster completed checking out Mr. Oaks, then headed back down to the street to hail a cab back to the port terminal.

On the shuttle into space, he looked back at the globe floating in space. Foster had read of an early scientist who proclaimed he could move a world with a long enough lever. Foster's secretive levers weren't long, but thanks to their invisibility they moved worlds nonetheless. As Valentia fell away beneath the shuttle, Foster finally allowed himself a small smile of satisfaction.

AUTHOR'S NOTE
STANDARDS OF SUCCESS

Back to the NASA space program, in particular the robotic rovers exploring Mars. Those rovers are remarkable achievements, and yet as the praise for them kept mounting I couldn't help noting how little they could actually do. The smallest tasks took days to complete and the smallest areas took days to creep across. An astonishing feat, yet extremely limited in what it could do and very slow in doing it. Humans on Mars could accomplish a lot more…if they were allowed to. After all, the extraordinary success of the robotic rovers had taught us how to best explore Mars. Right?

STANDARDS OF SUCCESS

26 March 2014 – The world today braced for the first landing of humans on Mars as NASA representatives declared that every possible step had been taken to ensure the safety and success of the mission. "NASA has adopted as its model the spectacularly successful unmanned missions to Mars, and will use similar operational methodology to maximize the results of this historic human mission. We want to duplicate to the greatest extent possible the amazing accomplishments of robotic explorers like the Spirit and Opportunity rovers while eliminating any possibility of even minor failures as a result of uncontrolled events."

NASA representatives repeated their previous statements that experience with unmanned missions led to the decision for scientists on Earth to control the landing on Mars, which in turn led to the extremely complex multiple-redundant landing system which neither requires nor allows any input from the astronauts actually riding in the Mars lander. "Experience with uncrewed probes dramatically highlighted the dangers to mission success of even a single input made without multiple layers of oversight to spot errors. In light of this experience, allowing a single, unsupervised astronaut to make inputs independently at critical points could put the entire mission at risk."

The official NASA press release points out that even though the astronauts have no way of themselves controlling their landing vehicle, if the crew of the Mars mission has any concerns during the landing sequence they need only contact NASA facilities on Earth, which would then take corrective action as quickly as needed, subject only to the ten minutes required for communications to reach Earth, the time required for a meeting involving all stake-holders in the mission to consider the situation and approve a course of action, and the ten minutes needed for any action agreed upon by the conference to be communicated back to Mars.

28 March 2014 – The first human landing on Mars yesterday was hailed as an outstanding achievement despite evidence that the landing vehicle came down in the wrong area due to a navigational error programmed into the system by operators on Earth. Confidential sources claim minutes and seconds of latitude and longitude for the landing site were plugged directly into the digital navigational system without converting them from base twelve to base ten, an error which went unnoticed by every layer of management review. "The important thing is that the mission landed safely," NASA representatives insisted, discounting concerns that the lander had missed falling into a deep canyon by only a small margin. NASA is refusing to release copies of transmissions from the lander on its final descent, which sources claim feature screams of terror from the astronauts.

12 April 2014 – NASA announced that after spending the last two weeks in preparation, the astronauts will begin standing up from their seats in the lander today as they continue to follow procedures developed during robotic missions. The standing up process, in which every movement will be monitored, is expected to take approximately one more week assuming all goes well.

18 April 2014 – Pleased NASA scientists declared that the astronauts on Mars had exceeded expectations by standing up from their seats in only six days. The next week will be spent checking the astronauts for problems before the process of moving the astronauts toward the lander hatch begins.

29 April 2014 – NASA announced that all three astronauts have been successfully lined up at the lander's exit hatch, a process

complicated by the need to coordinate each astronaut's movements from Earth to ensure none of them bumped into each other or any equipment inside the lander.

7 May 2014 – The first human step on the surface of Mars may be only hours away. Mission Commander Gus Grandin has spent the last several days on the ladder from the lander hatch to the Martian surface as each one of his steps was carefully planned and controlled by NASA scientists. He is currently paused on one leg with his right foot ten centimeters above the surface while NASA analyzes the implications of the discovery that a sixty centimeter diameter rock lies within one meter of the end of the ladder. NASA scientists, technicians and managers are currently debating whether to instruct Gus to step over the rock, maneuver around it, or abort the ladder sequence and return to the lander.

9 May 2014 – Gus Grandin became the first human to reach the surface of Mars today after he suffered from what NASA characterized as "involuntary muscle failure and/or spasms" after standing on one foot on the Mars lander ladder for the last two days while NASA attempted to decide on his best course of action. While celebrating the historic occasion, NASA warned that Gus appeared to be suffering from some undiagnosed problem which had led to "agitated" streams of conversation directed at NASA personnel. Technicians will attempt to remotely diagnose the cause of the problem and take corrective action. An anonymous source within NASA complained once again about the limitations of manned missions, noting that such a muscle failure would not have occurred in a robotic explorer. "Decisions shouldn't be forced as a result of short deadlines created by the limitations of the explorer mechanism."

16 May 2014 – All three astronauts have reached the surface of Mars not much more than a month and half after the landing. NASA technicians exchanged high fives after each astronaut successfully followed directions from earth controllers to maneuver

around the sixty centimeter diameter rock located near the end of the Mars lander ladder. According to plans, Mission Commander Gus Grandin will now extend one arm in order to hold a camera near the sixty centimeter diameter rock so that it can analyzed.

17 May 2014 – After an unexplained failure in Mission Commander Gus Grandin's arm, a back-up astronaut was ordered to extend an arm with a camera and hold it near the sixty centimeter diameter rock. An official NASA statement heralded the "remarkable string of results achieved thus far during the first human mission to the surface of Mars," noting that the astronauts had been able to stand up, climb down to the Martian surface, walk a distance of about one meter and begin some exploratory activity after just less than two months on the planet. This compares favorably, they noted, with the heralded achievements of robotic Mars probes about a decade ago.

18 May 2014 – NASA today scrambled to find an explanation for its loss of control over the Mars mission. After successfully and "nearly flawlessly" controlling the astronauts through their initial movements on the planet, reports indicate NASA personnel were shocked yesterday when the astronauts stopped responding to directions from Earth and began moving and acting independently. At the same time, what are officially characterized as "incomprehensible" transmissions have been received from the mission. Informed sources say the transmissions claim the astronauts completed the next six months of scheduled activities within the period of less than one hour after they ceased following orders from Earth.

The sources also state the astronauts are proceeding with further activities based upon their own observations instead of only executing experiments planned in great detail on Earth before being communicated to them.

Officially, NASA will only say that the mission "may be experiencing a mission command/response cycle malfunction which is impairing the effectiveness of the task input/task execution process."

NASA administrators publicly discount worries that the human astronauts may have gone 'rogue,' insisting that NASA will regain positive control of the astronauts in the near future. However, NASA personnel have privately conceded that if the astronauts continue to act independently, controlling their own actions and making their own decisions, it may imperil NASA's planned mission objectives and lead to unforeseen results. If this occurs, there may be no way to officially quantify the success of the mission. "This merely emphasizes the fact that sending humans into space creates risks to the successful completion of mission objectives above and beyond those seen in robotic missions," a senior NASA administrator noted.

"Exploration of the solar system is too important to let human astronauts create barriers to the future of humanity in space."

.

AUTHOR'S NOTE
THE BOOKSELLER OF BASTET

Wars do a lousy job of discriminating between those who want to fight and those who want to live in peace. The people and the ideas that make up the "collateral damage" in fighting might be worth paying attention to. Of course, that can also make them targets for those who don't want peace. I have always felt that those who sell and preserve books deserve a special place in society. They keep ideas, history and knowledge safe for the rest of us. That can sometimes be dangerous.

THE BOOKSELLER OF BASTET

The bookshop of Aaron D'abu filled to overflowing a ground level store space in the oldest building in Fraternity, the oldest city on the continent of Libertus on the world of Bastet. The bookshop had been there as long as the building and the city, its narrow street frontage only hinting at the deep space within, lined on both sides with shelves packed with every kind of book and magazine. E-readers and E-books in a hundred formats ranging from obsolete to not-quite-new cluttered one side, stacks of printed books filled the other, and in the very back against a wall covered with handbills announcing author readings and book signings rested an ancient Print On Demand console.

"When they founded this city," Aaron D'abu told me, "my grandfather, may his spirit be ever at peace, was told that the new land here needed hands to build and farm, not shops that sold words. He told them they were wrong, that it was words which had built all which humanity knew, and words which had brought us to this world far from the Earth our ancestors called home."

He waved toward the back of the store. "Look. Inside these walls we have the thoughts formed on Earth two or three thousand years ago and the latest imaginings of the newest generation here on Bastet. They rest side by side, for all books are companions to each other. So said my mother, may she also be at peace."

I'd come to Bastet on a diplomatic mission. Earth's children occupy many worlds now, but the mother feels responsibility for her offspring. There are still things the old mother can offer her children, perhaps the latest technology or new techniques for farming or even grants of devices which new worlds find prohibitively expensive to manufacture. It's all only a drop in the bucket, for even Earth can't do much measured against the needs of other worlds, but it grants the home world a bit of influence it might otherwise lack. Too little influence, it often seems, as we watch the new worlds make the same mistakes the old world once did.

How was business? I wondered, noticing that only a few locals were browsing among the many offerings in the bookstore.

"Not what it should be. Enough, but no more. Too many say they don't need these books," Aaron told me. "I tell them everything they want to know, someone else has thought or dreamed of, and it's all here for them to see. Would it kill them to learn of such thoughts? But, no, they claim to honor the past but don't care to learn from it because they say the future will be different." He waved a hand again, this time to encompass all around us. "Does this city look different? See here, the thoughts of the old religions, may all honor be to them. Next to them the new beliefs. Here the words of those who claim no god, and here the words of those whose gods are philosophy or money or power."

I asked him if he had any texts for the Anubans, who had declared themselves the only true children of the religion all Bastet had once shared. "Of course. You see? There with the others. Many say that the words of the Anubans as well as their people should be suppressed, but truth does not fear argument!"

In the cities to the north, I pointed out, bombs were going off as some Anubans fought for an independent state. "I live near Anubans! A nice family, who believe themselves chosen, but do not demand that everyone else submit to the same belief. I respect them." Aaron D'abu rummaged among his shelves. "See here. History. Wars and hatred, and for what? We're building a nice world here, for our children."

Did he have children?

"Alas, no. A nephew. He works here sometimes." Aaron sighed and offered me a seat at one of the beat-up tables lined down the middle of the bookstore. "My wife, blessed be her memory, died of the plague in twenty nine. You heard of it? An awful time. My nephew will have this store when I join her. People will always need books."

He chuckled and picked up a small battered disc from the floor. "Look at this! Cast aside, and yet it holds someone's story. Some writer's hopes. Look! A romance, I think." He studied the disc doubtfully. "I don't know if I have a reader that fits this anymore. It came from Earth with the first settlers. Do you think the one who wrote this ever dreamed it would travel to the stars and still be read so many years later?" Aaron smiled and carefully placed the possibly-unusable disc on a shelf piled high with a variety of other e-books and data holders.

He wasn't worried by the violence? One of the reasons our delegation was here was to try to broker a cease-fire, I explained. A few gestures of tolerance would deny the violent extremes of the Anubans most of their support.

"Blessings on your task," Aaron replied. "Worried? What can I do? I live with wisdom," he waved at the books again, "and am surrounded by human foolishness. Why would they hurt me? Who fears words?"

I didn't see Aaron D'abu again for a couple of months, being engaged in fruitless negotiations with the government and those who claimed to represent the Anuban sect. Eventually I returned to Fraternity and stopped by the bookseller again. He greeted me as if we'd just parted yesterday and this time offered refreshment. "It did not go well?"

No, I confessed, neither side wanted to be seen as giving in.

"If my mother were here, she would speak with them. In my mother's time," Aaron confided over a glass of hot, sweet tea, "the mayor of Fraternity was not a humble man. He thought himself wise above all and criticism angered him. One day, his police came to this very shop and pointed to a new book which mocked the mayor. Take it down, they said, or this shop will be closed."

"'Why should I remove this book?' my mother asked."

"'It is not truthful,' they told her."

"'Should I take down the book next to it, then?' my mother asked, which was a book saying good things about the mayor."

"'No,' they said, 'for that book is truthful.'"

"'But I must,' my mother declared, 'for the second book says the mayor is a fair and wise man, and such a man would not fear the words of those who disagree with him. If the mayor says I must hide such words, then the second book cannot be truthful, either.'"

Aaron D'abu grinned at me. "The mayor's police argued, then called their supervisor, who called her supervisor, and so on. The next day the mayor himself came and sat here, at this very table, and drank tea with my mother. She told him of all this store held and he listened, and then he told his police to leave her alone, because he who does not fear the truth does not fear lies. That was my mother."

He sighed and looked toward the back of the store. "She died there, seven years ago, among the words she treasured, taking inventory. It was as she wanted it. Her body was taken to the Garden of Memory but her spirit remains here."

Three months after that occasional bombs were going off in Fraternity. Tensions had kept rising, and both sides in the dispute were accusing we from Earth of favoring the other side instead of serving as honest brokers. A family had been massacred in a small town far to the north. Then two families in another town. Fighting began in Tvor City, radical Anubans striking and drawing retaliation against all Anubans, the radicals building support for themselves at the price of their own people's blood and the government hard-liners playing right into their hands.

Wisdom seemed in short supply when I next visited Fraternity and sought out Aaron D'abu. There were fewer people on the street than I remembered, and Aaron seemed saddened. "Some people leave, others hide. They say the war is coming. I once told you of neighbors I had, good people. But they received threats. Death to Anubans. And they left, for their children's sake. I could not blame them."

Had his business suffered?

Aaron sighed heavily. "Business is not even as good as it was. Not like in the old days. People now say they are too busy for books. Too busy to read, while the world gallops toward the abyss! Perhaps the words of others would give them pause, make them think, give them new eyes to see all around them. Or maybe they fear all that and so avoid it."

A sound of thunder rolled by and the shelves filled with books rattled slightly as if in momentary fright. The bookseller gazed out into the street, where a not-too-distant column of smoke could be seen rising over the buildings. "We came to this world, to this continent, to this city, to build things. And now too many just want to destroy what our mothers and fathers built. This will pass. I know it will. My books tell me it will. Another day will come." Aaron grimaced. "My nephew has been drafted. He will fight. When he comes home, he has promised to come work here."

Another few months and even the most optimistic among our delegation had to admit that we'd failed. Bombs were going off daily in cities and the death toll kept rising while both sides refused to compromise. Earth had no power to compel peace or reason, but was now being blamed in part for the ongoing violence, as if we could have somehow stopped what the people of this world seemed determined upon. We would leave, and try to see what we could accomplish elsewhere.

The decision was reached during a final meeting in Fraternity, so I resolved to say goodbye to Aaron D'abu before our delegation took its flight back to Bastet's spaceport the next morning. I'd finally buy some books from him, to help occupy the long trip to the next world on our schedule. As I walked toward the street on which his shop lay, I heard and felt and saw the explosion that rattled buildings all around me. Once I recovered, I started running, joining a crowd hastening to provide assistance.

The oldest building in Fraternity was no more. Only rubble remained of the structure. From the size and shape of the crater before it, a vehicle loaded with explosives had been detonated in front of the building.

I stumbled to a halt and stared at the devastation. Why?

I must have said the question out loud, because a woman beside me shook her head. "The building belonged to a man who now commands an anti-Anuban militia." She was crying, tears cutting paths through the bomb-birthed dust which had powdered her face. "Not ten minutes ago I came past here and greeted my friend Aaron. Have you ever noticed his bookstore?" I nodded. "All gone," the woman mourned. "Aaron and all he treasured. And for what? Aaron had been threatened by some Anubans. I knew of it. They didn't like some of the books he sold, but Aaron wouldn't take anything off the shelves. But look where they put the bomb! They didn't even care the bookstore was there. They just wanted to destroy the building."

And I truly didn't know at that moment which was worse; that people might deliberately destroy the bookshop of Aaron D'abu because they hated the ideas inside, or that they might heedlessly destroy it because they didn't care about the ideas it held.

"It's a task of great honor, to sell books," Aaron had once told me. "All of life, hope, death and love is within my walls. It's a great responsibility, you know. We booksellers, we come and go. But the books, the ideas, those remain with us always for those who seek them."

I left Bastet, wishing more people on that world had read the books which Aaron D'abu had once sold.

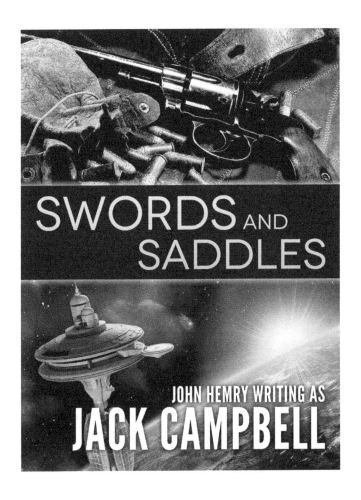

FOR NEWS ABOUT JABBERWOCKY BOOKS AND AUTHORS

Sign up for our newsletter*: http://eepurl.com/b84tDz
visit our website: awfulagent.com/ebooks
or follow us on twitter: @awfulagent

THANKS FOR READING!

Made in the USA
Las Vegas, NV
28 November 2022

60566395R00142